Hide And Seek

Hide And Seek

The Warrant Game

To Dick, aka The Judge!

Thanks for your support
and your good playing!

All the best!

Gary Smith
9/4/11

Gary Smith

E-mail = GSS10166@COMCAST.NET

Library of Congress Control Number: 2011904810
ISBN: Hardcover   978-1-4568-9267-8
           Softcover   978-1-4568-9266-1
           Ebook   978-1-4568-9268-5

This book was printed in the United States of America.

To order additional copies of this book, contact:
Xlibris Corporation
1-888-795-4274
www.Xlibris.com
Orders@Xlibris.com
81779

Acknowledgments

I wish to thank the men and women of the Los Angeles Police Department for their loyalty and attention to duty in a world that is getting more and more difficult with which to deal. It is a job that is highly underrated and misunderstood by many. Only those of us who have lived it truly know the realities of it. Thanks to the men with whom I served playing the Warrant Game of Hide and Seek. Special thanks to "Mel" my partner in the "Game" who put up with me and supported me in times of stress. Thanks also to Linda who lived through this part of my life with me and helped me with this story.

Many thanks to Ruthie who has been my inspiration and helper in getting my story on paper and for keeping the faith in my writing efforts.

Cover design by Rick Campbell Creative, Portland, Oregon.

Chapter One

He braced his pistol against the wooden frame of the barrier and waited. The S&W .38 started to feel heavy in his hand as he watched and waited for the man's silhouette to come into view. Suddenly, there it was, turned directly toward him. He squeezed the trigger. The pistol jumped in his hand as he fired five rounds. All five shots hit their intended marks.

"Reload in that position and holster your weapons," the range officer said over the loudspeaker. Pete Felix reloaded and holstered his weapon then picked up his shooting qualification receipt from the range officer and headed for the Los Angeles Police Department Academy restaurant.

Pete Felix was now pushing forty years old and had been a motorcycle officer for nearly sixteen years. He was starting to look like some of the old foot-beat cops he had worked with when he walked a beat in the Central Division of downtown Los Angeles back in the late 1950s. He still had all of his hair and hardly any wrinkles, but his belly now protruded a little over his beltline. At a little over five feet eight inches in height, he appeared to be stocky in his dark blue LAPD motor officer's uniform. He still had his now-famous sense of humor that had made him a lot of friends on the motor squad and a few police supervisors mad. Pete's antics at some of the motors roll calls had become legendary.

Now, he looked at his shooting score as he walked with one of the other cops who had just finished his monthly shooting qualification at the academy.

"Won't be long now and you won't have to qualify every month," commented the cop as he pointed to the three hash marks on Pete's motor officer's uniform sleeve. Those hash marks indicated that he'd been on the force for at least fifteen years or more, one hash mark for every five years of service. Pete would be adding his twenty-year mark in a few months.

"Yep," said Pete, "and I can hardly wait. Coming up here to the academy every month for almost twenty years gets to be a pain in the ass. But the food in the café is nice."

Actually, he enjoyed coming to the LAPD Academy, even though he was tired of shooting. Built in 1936, with the help of inmate labor and the iron hand of then Chief of Police James Davis, the academy was a part of the nostalgia of the earlier days of Los Angeles. The old tile-roofed Spanish buildings nestled between the hills of the Elysian Park were surrounded by palm and eucalyptus trees. Pete liked the aromatic odor that those trees and other vegetation covering the hills gave to the academy. He remembered what it had been like nearly twenty years ago, when he'd first come to the academy. Nearby Dodger Stadium hadn't existed then, and Chavez Ravine had been populated with Latino people. When the Dodgers came to town looking for a place to build a ballpark, the inhabitants were eventually removed one way or another. Some had gone peaceably, but a few had not. The difficulties had been big news in Los Angeles at the time, but finally the city had won out and the ball park had been built. Pete kinda liked it the way it had been before the Dodgers. He wasn't a baseball fan anyway.

As he walked, his mind wandered back to his days as a rookie in uniform in his first assigned area. Pete smiled to himself as his mind jumped back to one of his first learning experiences in the field after graduation from the academy. It was his fourth month working Central Division patrol and still on probation that all new cops must survive during their first year on the job. There were challenges.

Roll call that day back in 1959 had found Pete feeling really salty at the ripe old age of twenty-two. He felt he was learning a lot working the night watch in the big city.

"Smith and Mulroony, work 1A81." *Back to the west side*, thought Pete. *I love it.*

1A81 was a two-man car that had the area west from Figueroa to Commonwealth (the Central Division's border with the Hollywood Division) and the area between Sixth Street and Eleventh Street on the south border with the University Division. It was a high-crime area for burglaries, robberies, purse snatches, and drugs. Pete looked forward to the exciting possibilities of working there.

Bill Mulroony was a real old-timer. He had once been a motor cop, but the rumor was he got kicked off. He was a tall, slender man with dark hair and seemed very nervous.

They checked out a black-and-white 1957 Ford for their night's work. It was a real "junker." The city had purchased Fords in 1957. They were not really good for police vehicles, but they were durable. The cops hated them so much they tried to blow the engines up by misusing them. The problem was that those underpowered six-cylinder engines that wouldn't "pull a sick whore off a piss pot" wouldn't blow up!

Bill was driving as they cleared for duty with communications and headed west on Sixth Street. It was dusk, and the sun was almost down. As they approached Central Receiving Hospital at Columbia Street, Bill swerved into the left-hand lane and started to brake hard. Pete thought he must have seen a crime or a suspect. Pete's adrenalin started to pump.

"It's Bubbles," Bill yelled. He made a screeching U-turn and drove east, the way they had just come. "There she is!" He made another screeching *U* and pulled up to the curb. A tall, not very good-looking woman in her mid-twenties was walking down the sidewalk. Then he saw them! She had the largest breasts Pete had ever seen in his life! They were pushing very hard on the inside of a very tight sweater.

"Hey, Bubbles!" Bill yelled. "Com'ere."

The "boobs that walked" approached Pete's side of the car and leaned over to his level. Pete was speechless. He was also still on probation.

Bill said, "Get in the back seat."

Now the boobs in the back seat pointed right at Pete!

"Hey, Pete, feel those beauties. Go ahead."

Bubbles moved closer so Pete could reach over the seat. He was torn between good sense and wanting to be one of the guys. He grabbed one of the prizewinners. *Honk, honk!*

"All right," said Pete under his breath, "let's get out of here, Bill!"

"Hey, Bubbles, how 'bout a blow job?"

Now Pete was starting to panic! *How do I get out of this without being a sissy?* he thought wildly. I could lose my job over something like this! His mind raced to think of an answer.

"No," said Bubbles, "I got to go somewhere to meet my cousin."

"Oh, come on. This won't take long," Bill pleaded.

"Well, okay, if you don't mind getting orange lipstick on your dick."

Now Bill was driving around looking for a dark alley near where they were. *It's not even dark yet!* Pete thought to himself. *Oh God!* The police radio saved the day.

"1A81, 1A81. A possible 211 in progress, [the address], 1A81 the call is code 2."

"Shit, Bubbles. We gotta go handle that call," moaned Pete's partner.

They dropped Bubbles off on the corner and went to the call.

"Too bad," said Pete, laughing to himself and feeling very relieved. The call turned out to be a phony, and Bill was really disappointed. Pete wanted to yell hallelujah!

As the evening wore on, Pete found out more about Bill. He was on medication for his stress problems. He told Pete about his marital problems and about his former wife, a Los Angeles policewoman whom he had caught in the arms of another policewoman lover. *I guess that would shake me up too,*

Pete admitted to himself. He felt sorry for him, but he thought he wouldn't want to work with him again, if he had a choice in the matter.

Pete's mind then jumped ahead a few years to when he had made the cut to be a motorcycle officer. Some of his antics bordered on insubordination, but he survived due to the humor it brought to the other motor cops. Like the time he walked into the roll call room when the captain was giving out Safe Riding Award tie bars. Pete had never received one as yet in his first few years on motors.

He resented some of the officers who did get them, many of which never took risks to catch speeders or chased violators too fast. There were several cops that he had worked with that only wrote the easy tickets like jaywalking and other simple low risk offenses. Pete had several minor accidents while on duty that were blamed on him as "preventable." To him, that seemed to be the result of his aggressive attitude when enforcing traffic violations. The chase was still exciting for him, but it didn't earn him any safety awards.

Just before one of the Safe Riding Award roll call sessions, Pete contacted one of the officers who had gone down in an accident on the freeway and had skidded quite a ways on his uniform. Pete borrowed the uniform that was in tatters on the knees, with the seat of the breeches hanging in shreds, and put them on before roll call. After the captain had started to give his big talk on riding safety, Pete made his entrance in the tattered uniform. The cops in the room roared with laughter as Pete sat down with his knees exposed.

"Pretty cute, Felix," stated the captain, trying not to appear mad. But all the cops knew he was seething. "Why don't *you* come up here and give out the awards, Felix?"

So Pete took him up on the offer and made a lot of fun out of the ceremony by awarding the laziest officer the "Slow-Riding Safety Award." Another officer got the award for surviving the most "slow-speed wobbles." It was a riot for the cops, and the captain couldn't say anything because it would not look good for him as their supervisor not to have a motor officer sense of humor. Pete had gotten away with a lot of stunts during his time on the motor squad that had made him well liked by his peers. Most of the supervisors tolerated him. Several did not.

One arrogant lieutenant whom Pete had labeled "Elf Ears" got upset at some of Pete's remarks one day and pulled him into his office after roll call.

"Felix, I don't want to hear another word out of you at roll call! Understand?"

"Yes, sir," said Pete with a military salute.

The next day at roll call, the lieutenant called roll. "Johnson?" "Here." "McKinney?" "Here, sir." "Felix?" No answer. "Felix!" No answer. "FELIX!" From the back of the room came a muffled sound: Mmmmmm! The lieutenant looked for the sound; he saw Pete with a large piece of duct tape covering his mouth!

"Take that tape off your mouth and answer up, Felix," yelled the lieutenant.

Pete removed the tape and yelled back, "But, sir, you told me not to say another word at roll call. I was just making sure I followed your orders." The room fell apart with loud guffaws, and the day was made for most of the cops. Pete loved to agitate the supervisors that were not well liked by the men.

Pete came out of his reverie as he walked into the academy restaurant and looked around. A hand waved at him from a corner table. The hand belonged to one of his old partners, Bill Haymes. Pete and Bill had graduated from the motor officer training school together and worked as partners for about five years as Big City Motor Cops (BCMCs). They broke up when Bill was promoted to sergeant in 1967 and had to leave motors. Now he was a lieutenant in the Records and Identification Division (R&I), where the department kept all of its crime and arrest records and warrants. Pete had kept in touch with his ex-partner through the years.

Bill was tall and dark, with a salt and pepper mustache and a slightly receding hairline. Pete headed over to join his old partner at his table.

"Hey, Sweets," greeted Pete, using the old nickname he had given Bill years ago. The two cops shook hands, and Pete sat down.

"What's happening, Crash?" asked Bill. "How many times have you fallen off your motorcycle this week?"

"At least I reported my accidents, which is more than I can say for some people I know. But fortunately, the statute of limitations has run out." They both chuckled as they exchanged the ritual greeting insults that cops go through when they meet.

"Man, I'm doin' my monthly duty blowin' up a paper target. How are things up there in squintland?" asked Pete. The word *squint* referred to any cop who got out of the field for one reason or another. Most street cops felt that any job that wasn't directly involved in making arrests or investigation of crimes was a "squint job."

Bill chuckled at Pete's derogatory remarks. He was used to them after all those years. "Man, I'm learning all kinds of things. There *is* life after motors."

"It's a good thing you made sergeant. You weren't worth a shit as a motor cop," said Pete with a twinkle in his eye. Of course, he really thought Bill had been a pretty good motor cop, and Pete had learned a lot while they were partners. In fact, the two had learned from each other. Bill had taught Pete the value of patience and maturity in doing police work. Pete had taught Bill humor and how to use it in dealing with people. Although they differed greatly in personality, they were good friends.

After a few minutes of catch-up on each other's lives, Pete changed the subject. "I'm gettin' real fed up with workin' the field in uniform. It ain't the same anymore. Seniority doesn't mean shit, and since Traffic Enforcement Division (TED) was decentralized, our supervisors now are guys who mostly never worked motors. And you know what that means."

"Yeah, it means you can't get away with the bullshit we used to get away with in TED," said Bill smiling at his friend. "It's a whole new ball game, Pete. The world is changing."

"I kinda liked it the way it was. You know, kicking ass and takin' names and putting assholes in jail."

"I'd think after almost twenty years of being a street cop, you'd want a change. Don't you get tired of writing tickets?"

"I don't know," said Pete. "Sometimes I think about it, then I bust someone who really needs to go to jail, and I feel good and like what I'm doin'."

"You need to get out of uniform and let the young, hard chargers get out and do the dirty work."

"That's what scares me. Have you seen the 'hard chargers' lately? My God, these guys are more concerned about getting their degrees and buying sailboats and motor homes than doing police work!"

Bill chuckled. "That's because you look at things as if this were the quest for the Holy Grail or something. This is a job."

"Blasphemy! Chief Parker is turnin' over in his grave!"

"I guess there's no hope for you. But you'll have to start thinking about what you'll do when it's time to retire."

That thought was one Pete avoided. He knew he would have to sooner or later. *Later*, he thought. He changed the subject. "What have you been up to lately?"

"Right now, I'm working on a project that's revolutionized the department's record-keeping responsibility. LA County and LA City have consolidated the database for criminal records and fingerprint files. It's all been automated with computers. The county and city are working together to update the whole record-keeping system. It's a huge undertaking, and I'm right in the middle of it."

"Sounds interesting," said Pete. "What's your job?"

"I helped to coordinate and implement the system. It's a long story, but the bottom line is now we can access records much quicker and cheaper than we used to. Remember when it used to take ten to fifteen minutes to get a record check from R&I?"

"Yeah, while we waited out there in the cold and the violator got pissed off."

"Right. That's because R&I had to search the files by hand whenever we wanted information on a suspect. Then, if the suspect had a warrant, remember how long it used to take to get it teletyped to a jail?"

"At least thirty minutes," remembered Pete.

"You're right. Those things have improved 100 percent. We can run a license plate while we're rollin' and get an answer in a few seconds now. It's a good deal."

"Well, I've been responsible for implementing the whole program for LAPD and working with the LA Sheriff's Department on the project."

"Sounds like a lot of work. So now you're in R&I running the show."

"Well, not exactly. I'm second in command."

"I'm impressed. Say, how about a job for me up there?" Pete said jokingly. Then he thought, *Why not?*

"Are you serious? There are a couple of openings on the Warrant Detail up there."

Pete remembered that serving arrest warrants was a job given to motor cops when rain curtailed safe operation of motorcycles on Los Angeles' slippery streets. BCMCs went out in cars and attempted to serve arrest warrants that had been issued from the courts. Compared to riding, it was boring as he remembered. But it was a way to put criminals in jail and keep motor cops busy until the rain stopped.

"I don't know. Let me think about it," said Pete. "The cut in pay if I left motors is something I have to figure out. Those extra hundred dollars a month comes in handy. Plus I would lose my ride to work as well."

"Well, let me know soon before the openings go away." Pete said good-bye to his friend and headed back to his motorcycle.

That evening, Pete mentioned the subject to his wife. Noel Felix was an attractive forty-year-old woman with blond hair and a very good shape for her age. Pete and Noel had been married about ten years now. It had been the second marriage for Noel. Her first marriage had produced two sons, Richard and Michael. Both boys lived with Pete and their mother. They were fifteen and fourteen years old, respectively.

"I thought you loved motors and were gonna stay there until you retire?" said Noel with a somewhat incredulous look on her face. She knew how much Pete loved riding motorcycles and doing police work. She couldn't picture him as doing anything else. She also remembered the time she had been driven to the hospital by one of Pete's fellow officers when Pete had been hit by a car while he was chasing another violator. That accident had broken both of Pete's ankles and his arm. Like many other cops' wives, she had lived with the constant fear for her husband's life as a police officer. Now, here was a chance for her husband to get away from a part of the job that she hated. Inwardly she hoped he would take the opportunity to get off motors, but she would never say that to Pete.

"Well, I'm starting to think I'm bustin' my ass for nothing on motors. Besides, it isn't fun anymore. We used to put the bad guys in jail and feel like we were doin' something. Now, the assholes are back on the street before we are finished with the paperwork it took to put 'em in! Besides, Bill Haymes is a lieutenant up there in R&I, and there is an opening for an officer to serve arrest warrants."

"What would be the difference in what you're doing now and the new job serving warrants?"

"I would lose my motorcycle-riding hazard pay and the transportation to and from work. But the thought of hunting down people who have skipped bail or are wanted for crimes is kinda exiting to me."

"Think about it. Most of the people cops bust get out on bail. A lot of them split and don't return to court. Of the ones who do, many don't pay their fines and have arrest warrants out for them. So I started thinking it would be an important job to hunt down the ones who slip through the court system or who don't do their time or pay their fines. It would be like a game of hide-and-seek with the bad guys."

Noel noticed the spark of enthusiasm in his voice and in his eyes and knew he had made up his mind. She permitted herself a little internal smile of relief.

Later that evening, Pete and Noel were entertaining a neighbor couple and the subject came up about seeing his old partner, Bill, and about the warrant job.

"I know police serve warrants. What? Like search warrants? How do warrants work anyway?" asked Tom Carreon, who lived next door. "I've heard of search warrants but never really understood about other types of warrants."

Pete explained it as best he could.

"Warrants are issued by the courts that direct police to arrest a person or take property into custody."

"You mean like, a judge signs warrants?" asked Ginger, Tom's wife.

"Right. Warrants can be for major or minor offenses. On one end of the spectrum, a warrant could be issued for failure to pay a traffic ticket. On the other end, it could be for murder or some other serious crimes."

"Oh, there are different grades of warrants?" said Tom.

"Yep. See, arrest warrants are divided into two classes: felonies and misdemeanors. Felony warrants are for serious crimes, such as murder, rape, kidnapping, robbery, and other heavy stuff like that. Felony warrants are good for many years, and they can be served on the person named on the warrant anytime of the night or day. Misdemeanor warrants are more restricted in the time they can be served because they relate to minor crimes like petty theft, minor drug-use violations, drunken-driving offenses, failure to pay child support, and a lot of other relatively minor offenses, as compared to felonies."

"How do cops serve warrants?" asked Ginger.

"Most of the time they don't," Noel chimed in.

"That's right," said Pete. "See, most cities don't spend too much time searching for people wanted on misdemeanor warrants, even though tons of money is lost by the state and by those who put up bail. Most of those warrants that do get served wind up being served on people by chance. For example, say a cop stops a person for a traffic violation or some suspected criminal activity and runs a record check of police files on the individual. Any wants or warrants would usually come to light and the person is arrested on the warrant. We take them 'before a magistrate,' which means 'to jail,' where they're booked and allowed to put up bail. That is *if* we catch 'em."

"What about if they don't get caught . . . 'by chance,' as you say?" asked Tom.

"Some police organizations like the LAPD, the LA County Sheriff, and the LA County Marshal's Office have special units that serve warrants just like bounty hunters. Only, these guys get paid by the city or county they work for as just a part of their job. Millions of dollars of taxpayers' money are lost every year by failure to collect legally assessed fines. Some people don't pay because they can't. Others don't pay because they won't. Then it becomes a game of 'hide-and-seek.' A hell of a lot of people are hiding and very few cops are seeking 'em."

After the neighbors had left, Pete wondered if they really understood what he had told them. He remembered the conversation he had with another friend when he was questioned about just being a cop and how it had affected his life.

Several years ago, Pete was out on the desert doing some off-road riding with his old buddy, Mack McCune. After a long, cool morning ride, the sun had started to beat down and the temperature climbed to the point where riding became uncomfortable. At that time, the riders parked their motorcycles and had some cold beer under the awning they set up and smoked cigars and talked.

"Mind if I ask you a personal question?" asked Mack.

"Like what?" Pete answered, blowing cigar smoke into the air.

"Don't take this the wrong way because we've been friends for a long time. I wondered how being a cop has affected your life. I mean, the way you feel about things now that you've been a cop for a while."

"Well, let's see. It gets kinda complicated, and a lot of people don't understand, but let me try to answer your question." Pete took a big swig of his beer.

"Being a cop and dealing with the law and the judicial system makes you start thinking in a more legalistic way. It makes it harder to communicate with friends you knew before you joined the force. You start to change, at least in the eyes of others. You develop a different attitude and approach to things. I'm not saying it's a bad change. In some ways, it may seem to be from others' points of view, but the changes are necessary ones to a cop. Without them, a cop cannot survive."

"What do you mean 'survive'?" Mack asked.

"You gotta be able to think clearly what to do in every situation you're in. Your decisions must be based on the law, and they must be quick. You gotta be able to walk into a call for police service and take command and responsibility for the situation. You have to let the people know you are in charge. They must have confidence in you. You have to be firm, but fair. You must be ready to use force when it is required, and you can't lose! If you lose, you may be dead."

"That's a pretty large order to fulfill, isn't it?"

"Damn right! It changes you. It makes you less tolerant of some things and more of others. It allows you to cut through a lot of people's bullshit and see them as they really are. That's not always what you want to see. It makes you want to take action when most people would look the other way. It makes you fully aware that there is a cold, hard world out there with a lot of cold people in it who will kill you only because you wear a blue uniform. Then the bad guy goes home and sleeps like a baby that night. You discover that there are people who will rob and beat an elderly woman and take her last cent. People who will lie every time their lips move. It also makes you thankful for what you have and how you live."

"I bet you've seen a lot of bad things in your job, right?"

"One of the hardest parts is seeing the way some people live. It's a real eye-opener. To those of us who have been brought up in middle-class America in good homes, it's hard to realize how some people can live like they do. You realize that most people are not very clean or honest. They fight about stupid things and are too quick to try to settle things by violence. You lose what tolerance you may have had with intoxicated people. You develop a strong disgust for dopers, dealers, and prostitutes."

"That sounds like the way most honest people feel. But I guess most of us don't see that side of life every day."

"True, and the effects of these experiences begin to show up in your personality. Friends don't understand what it is or why. They only see you as a 'badge-heavy cop.' They think you are trying to act tough or something. Your sense of humor undergoes a change. Then one day you realize that you can't change the world. You can't even change people. You have to deal with the world the way it is and accept it the way it is or you will be overcome by it."

"I thought when I first met you, you were kinda strange," Mack said as he laughed. Pete went on.

"You begin to understand why policemen laugh about the predicaments that people get themselves in and the pain and violence they bring on themselves. If you can't laugh about it, you will cry about it and be unable to do the job that has to be done. That job is to protect and serve the people of LA. The way cops do it is to put the people who break the laws in jail. Let the social workers and reformers do their thing their way, but someone has to get the real assholes off the street."

"Too bad people can't just obey the law and stay out of trouble," said Mack as he puffed his cigar. Pete perceived a hint of humor in Mack's remark and smiled.

"Most people don't realize that society is like constructing a building. The cops are down at the bottom, protecting the foundation so the rest of the building can go up. If the foundation is cut away or weakened enough, the whole building will come down. Of course, the people up above don't understand what's going on down below. All they see is their particular part of the construction job or maintenance job. A policeman understands the importance of his job too well. That's what makes it so hard on him."

"He sees the rotten part of our society and hopes and prays it will not affect his family or loved ones. He also wants to protect those who are the innocent victims of the scum. They can't protect themselves. The strong or wicked will always prey on the weak and helpless. Our 'modern' society will not allow people to defend themselves except in extreme instances. Some people think that even the police go too far. Sometimes they do. Sometimes it is necessary in order to show the scum that all society is not weak and afraid of them."

Mack frowned and said, "Seems to me that most of the bad guys get right back out of jail and onto the street nowadays!"

"Cops know how the system of 'justice' works in today's America. It is rapidly bogging down in a legal system where justice is not swift or just many times. The victims are the ones who are nearly always ignored. Let me tell you this story that woke me up a lot."

Mack leaned forward to hear better.

"One night, when I was a rookie cop working the old Central Division in downtown Los Angeles, we got a call to the old Bunker Hill section of town. Bunker Hill was at one time a very fashionable part of Los Angeles. It took in the area surrounded by Hill Street on the east, Flower Street on the west, Fourth Street on the south, and First Street on the north. The Angel's Flight cable car operates up the hill from Third and Hill to the top. The houses were built before the turn of the century and were now old and run-down. They were mostly occupied by pensioners and prostitutes.

"My partner and I arrived at this old apartment building and were met by an elderly woman about eighty years old. She lived in a dirty apartment for which she paid rent from her Social Security check. She barely survived this way. She had saved her pennies for several years to buy a TV set. She couldn't get out much and the TV was her only recreation and contact with the rest of humanity."

Mack is very interested by now.

"One day, not long after she bought her TV set, the little old lady was out to the store down the street. While she was gone, some scumbag broke into her apartment and stole her TV. We took the 459 burglary report. My partner and I discussed the way things would probably happen when and if the suspect was caught. It went something like this."

"The burglar would go to jail for a little while then bail out. While out on bail he would continue to rob the weak. The old lady would still be without her TV set because she couldn't afford to buy another one. A pretrial hearing would be set and the old lady would have to attend. No one would bring her to court. She would have to make it on her own. When she gets there, she will find that the defendant has the services of the public defender, who asks for and receives a continuance so he and the scumbag can prepare his defense. The old lady finds her way home. The case comes up again. Same routine. The defense is hoping the old lady will die so the case will be dropped. The strategy is to keep the case coming back again and again and weaken the case. Does the judge know this? Probably not. He's got other things to worry about. Individual problems are not his concern."

Pete took a deep breath and continued. "Finally, if we are lucky, scumbag will be convicted and he will go to the hands of the probation department. There, some well-meaning young college graduate whose head has been filled with a bunch of bullshit by some not-so-well-meaning college professor will try to help this poor soul who has been a victim of our capitalistic society and never had a chance because of racial prejudice or he has a 'substance dependency' and not a drug addict or dope fiend. The poor man must be 'understood' and we must try to rehabilitate him. The scumbag loves it because he can make these dumb bastards believe anything. What about the victim? The little old lady? Oh, she died not long after the scumbag went to the Honor Farm. She didn't get to watch any TV either."

The next shooting qualification day at the academy, Pete ran into another of his former motor officer partners.

"I'm thinkin' about gettin' off motors," Pete said to his other ex-motor partner seated across the table from him in the Police Academy restaurant. Ron Byron sipped his coffee and smirked at his old partner.

"You'll die on motors," sneered Byron. "You love writing those chicken-shit tickets too much. You should have left a long time ago, like I did."

"Yeah, like you," laughed Pete, "and become a squint and shuffle geek at the academy."

"I'm goin' up the ladder of success to higher things," said Ron in an exaggerated tone and an upward hand gesture.

"Right." Pete put his right index finger in his nostril, pretending to pick his nose. "I used to couldn't spell *sarjent*, now I are one," he chided.

Ron had left motors over a year before and transferred to the Training Division at the academy where he now coordinated the police recruits' training. His job was to keep track of the recruits and to intimidate them, just like he had been intimidated when he went through the academy. Ron did a good job of that. He had shaved his head of what little hair was left, which gave him an even more stern appearance. He inspected the troops every morning and got them off to their classes, as well as kept track of their progress or the lack of it.

"I'm gettin' real tired of being kicked around out in the field," Pete whined. "I always looked forward to having seniority so I could get weekends off and a good vacation time, for a change. Now that I finally get some seniority, they say seniority doesn't mean anything. Hell, I remember when the old-timers got all weekends off while we worked. Now, no one can remember all that."

"You know why it's that way, don't you?"

Pete stared at his friend, waiting for his comment.

"Because that's the way it is."

"Thanks for the eye-opener, asshole," said Pete.

"That's 'Officer Asshole,' if you please. Anyway, seniority is old-fashioned, haven't you heard?" said Ron.

"I've been talking to Bill Haymes in Records and Identification Division. He's a lieutenant up there. You remember him from our motors training class? He says a couple of guys are getting ready to retire. It's a P-2 spot and I qualify. I asked around and the job sounds pretty good. You work only weekdays during business hours, every weekend off, plain clothes, and not much supervision. Most of the guys up there are old-timers. Sounds great to me."

"Sounds boring to me."

"What could be more boring than having to deal with these immature, undisciplined little whip dicks who all want to save the planet?" exclaimed Pete. "Anyway, I'd still be out in the field putting assholes in jail."

"You'll never leave motors. You'll die there." Ron really believed it.

Chapter Two

Pete walked into the squad room of the Warrant Detail at 6:30 a.m. on the first day of his new job. The thing that hit him immediately was that this was not exactly a room. It was a small corner of the record storage area on the mezzanine floor of the Police Administration Building (PAB) at Parker Center. The squad room area was formed by a wall of filing cabinets on two sides and a real wall on the rear. The front was open to the rest of the civilian workers in that room. The rest of the large room was filled with civilian employees working at computers and filing documents.

Pete looked around the so-called office *room* and saw there were two rows of long tables serving as desks, making a working space for up to fifteen officers. The sergeant who supervised the detail had his own desk separate from the others. The cops worked in teams of two, and each team had a phone. The new guy could see that there were about six officers already on duty.

The men who worked the unit continued to straggle in, one by one. Pete knew a couple of them.

"Hey, Petey," yelled Billy Much. Pete had worked with Billy in patrol back at Central Division when they were both rookies. A black officer named D. J. Willis came in. He had also worked Central at that time. Several others in the unit looked familiar to Pete. All were seasoned officers. Bobby Gomez was the youngest man in the unit. He had seven years on the job and was a Vietnam vet. He looked mean. Pete greeted each man and shook hands, introducing himself to those he didn't know.

"Well, that's all we need. A crazy motor jockey in the unit." Pete looked at the older man who had just made the comment. He recognized Ed Newell as an old-timer he'd seen around for years. Pete had always thought the guy was a detective.

"What's the matter, Pops? Afraid I'll park in the space where you park your electric wheelchair?" said Pete. The older cop frowned as the other guys in the unit laughed.

"Not too funny, dickhead," said Ed.

"The name is Peter, like what you used to have between your legs before it shriveled up and fell off," said the younger officer with a smile. More laughter from the troops.

"Don't try matching wits with this guy, Ed. I've heard stories about him and his antics at those motors roll calls," said Billy. Pete made a mental note to thank Billy for the help. The older man, whom Pete christened "Uncle Ed," had just lost his longtime partner to retirement. Uncle Ed, who was closing in on retirement himself, really didn't want a new partner. But that was Pete's new job! Being Uncle Ed's new partner!

"I'll check out the car, kid. I drive," advised Uncle Ed. *Fine with me*, thought Pete. *Now I'm a forty-year-old kid!* The two reluctant partners walked down to the garage parking area to get their car. Pete, who didn't smoke, also noticed that Uncle Ed smoked heavily. *Great! Nothing like spending all day in a police car with a smoke stack*, he thought. They got into a dark green unmarked Chevy car that wouldn't have fooled anyone on the street. *We might as well blow a siren*, thought Pete.

As Pete started to write down the odometer mileage on the daily field activities log, Uncle Ed shifted into reverse and screeched the rear tires as he backed out of the parking place. Pete's pen slid off the page! After jerking to a stop, Ed shifted the automatic transmission into drive and mashed his foot on the accelerator. *Screeech!* The tires spun again as the car lunged forward. *This is going to be fun*, thought Pete.

They spent the early part of that first day jerking around from house to house in the Seventy-seventh Division. Pete's duties seemed to consist of getting out of the car by himself and placing notices of warrants on several doors where no one was home. After a couple of hours of that, Uncle Ed informed Pete that he had several very important personal errands that needed to be run. Important things like buying liquor at a place on the west side of town because they gave him a discount then a trip to the party supply store for stuff for a party his girlfriend was throwing.

A few days of this fantastic Newell-Felix partnership made it clear to Pete that the first day had been Uncle Ed's standard for a good day's work.

After three or four more days, Ed got generous and allowed Pete to drive the police vehicle. As Uncle Ed was just about to start the log, Pete put the car into reverse and spun the tires backing up and then peeled out down the aisle, copying Uncle Ed's performance behind the wheel. As they pulled up to the gas pumps for fuel, Uncle Ed was fuming!

"Goddammit, kid! If you're gonna drive like an idiot, I'm gettin' out right here," said he sputtered. Pete was laughing so hard he could hardly reply.

"You fucking old fart! I'm driving just exactly the way you've been driving every day!" exclaimed Pete, banging his hands on the steering wheel and laughing hysterically.

"Bullshit!" said Uncle Ed. "I'm not ridin' with you if you're gonna drive like that." Pete had made his point though and casually went back to his normal pattern of driving sanely. Ed seemed to drive a little better after that too.

Uncle Ed was not highly motivated to do any arresting of wanted people. Especially if he had to walk up any stairs or to use the least bit of energy in any way, except for shopping! Pete was really bummed out and was beginning to think he may have made a big mistake in leaving motors.

Mel Tennesen had about fifteen years on the job. He'd become a cop at an older age than most cops. The average age of a police recruit is about twenty-two or twenty-three. Mel had been twenty-nine when he received his appointment to the academy. That made him about four years older than Pete but with less time on the job. Mel had spent four years in the Marine Corps before coming on the job. He seemed like a quiet and mild-mannered guy. Pete liked him immediately.

"Mel," said Pete as they walked out of the back door toward the police cars. "I hear old Uncle Ed is retiring soon. When he does, how about teaming up with me?" Mel's current partner was also retiring to become a prison guard.

"Sure, Pete. I think we'd make a good team." They shook on it and teamed up as partners as soon as Uncle Ed retired.

The two new partners were like night and day in personality. Pete, the outgoing extrovert who always had a wisecrack remark about everything and everyone. Mel, quiet, somewhat introverted. They also had other differences. Mel was a jock! He ran marathons, raced bicycles, and ate health food. His body was trim, and he looked younger than his years.

Pete, on the other hand, only ran when being chased, wouldn't be caught dead on a bicycle, and ate as much junk food as he could. His body had developed that "old-timer" look with his belly protruding slightly over his belt. Despite their differences, they had one thing in common: the desire to do police work! Where Uncle Ed was incapable of doing a day's work, Pete and Mel enjoyed the game of "hide-and-seek" they played with wanted suspects.

They agreed early in the partnership to monitor the police car radio, if the car had one, or check out a hand-held radio and respond to emergency calls for police service or to back up patrol officers. The majority of other men in the unit weren't interested in listening to the radio and almost never got involved in street police work. To them, the warrant unit was a place to *retire*. Pete and Mel didn't feel that way. Pete still had that urge to be out there doing police work. Many of the old-timers and some of the newer officers didn't understand that urge. Mel did.

Although he'd been in the unit for several weeks now, Pete had only started to learn his new job. Uncle Ed had no interest in teaching him anything about the job. He'd been just biding his time until he retired. Pete felt somewhat embarrassed asking basic questions about the job, but Mel, who had been in the unit for about five years, was glad to explain the rules of hide-and-seek to his new partner.

"Here's how we play the game," explained Mel. "As you know, the green warrant abstracts we call 'greenies' are sent to us. The hard copies of the warrants are in the files here in R&I. We can arrest and book a person on the greenies, and the clerks dig out the hard copies before the defendant goes to court. We catch 'em, transport 'em to the closest LA city jail, and book 'em. No reports are necessary unless we have a problem. We don't even have to advise them of their Miranda Rights on a warrant arrest. We have countywide jurisdiction. That means we can go anywhere in LA County and arrest. We're supposed to notify the local police jurisdiction when we're in another town looking for suspects, but usually we don't."

"What about these prisoner pickups I hear you guys talking about?" asked Pete. It was like his first day in the unit, and Pete mentally cursed Uncle Ed for not taking the time to teach his new partner anything.

"Our unit is also responsible for picking up prisoners in other cities or other parts of California who have been arrested on our warrants. If there's a warrant out on a person here and that person moves up to San Francisco and gets busted up there on our warrant, they notify us. We have five days to pick the person up and bring his ass—or hers—back to court in LA. If we don't pick them up within the time limit, they kick 'em loose, and the game starts over again." Pete listened intently.

"We don't mess with felony warrants. That's the Fugitive Detail's job. And we don't go out of state. Misdemeanor warrants are only good for daytime service in our state. That means sunup to sundown. No night service. We can work weekends if we want to, but no one wants to, so we don't," explained Tennesen. "We watch our ass just as if the guys on the misdemeanor warrants were felons though. You never know what you're getting into when you knock on the door in this game."

"Thanks, Mel. I'll remember that."

Pete's new career field brought back some memories of his early days in Central Division Patrol, where he had spent the first two and a half years before becoming a motor officer. During that time, he had experienced many calls for police service that required him to go into people's homes and apartments. He was stunned at first by the way some people live.

Having grown up in a middle-class family in Iowa in a modest but clean environment, he had never seen the darker side of the lives of some people. On one of his first calls as a rookie, he and his partner went to a small apartment house near MacArthur Park, another rundown area of Los Angeles. The manager met the officers at the door.

"What's the trouble?" asked Pete, the rookie.

"This guy who rents here has been in his room for days now and hasn't come out, and he makes funny noises now and then. I got worried that maybe he was sick or even dead! So I called you guys." This was enough reason for the officers to enter the apartment to investigate as to the welfare of the occupant.

"Do you have a pass key?" Pete's partner asked.

"Yeah. I'll open the door." The manager unlocked the door and swung it open.

"Holy shit!" coughed Pete as the smell hit the officers in the face like a hot breeze. The odor in the room was indescribable! A mixture of feces, urine, alcohol, and God knows what else! The officers knew what needed to be done but hated the idea of doing it.

"Here's the deal, Pete. We flip a coin and whoever loses goes in and checks to see if this poor bastard is still alive." Pete agreed and crossed his mental fingers.

The coin went up and down and Pete lost. "I knew it!" Pete whined. Taking a deep breath and holding it, Pete entered the room and went to the foot of the bed on which the man lay. Kicking the foot of the bed, Pete yelled, "Hey! Wake up!" He realized quickly that you can't yell and hold your breath at the same time and Pete ran back out into the hallway to get another breath of fresh air.

The officers were finally able to get the semi comatose alcoholic to a state of consciousness enough to get him off to the hospital for medical treatment.

"Whoa, let's go get some coffee and a greasy doughnut so I can get the taste of that room out of my nose and mouth!" said Pete to his partner. He never forgot the incident. There were others, but none ever matched the first one. Mel and Pete's areas of responsibility included entering many sleazy homes and apartments while looking for warrant suspects. Some were not just dirty but strange as well.

Mel pulled out a warrant greenie for a man whose last address was in an area in which Pete worked as a patrol cop. They drove to the location in the Silver Lake area near downtown Los Angeles. Silver Lake is the name of a large reservoir from which the area takes its name. In the old days, that area was the home of many famous Hollywood actors and directors. Now, it was mostly inhabited by homosexuals and low-class residents.

The address on the warrant was a house built on the side of a hill, and there were about twenty steps leading down to a side entrance. Mel knocked and a middle-aged woman answered the door.

"We are Los Angeles police," said Mel, and both officers showed their police ID cards to the woman. "Is Donald Conway home?"

"He's my son. What the trouble?"

"Sorry, ma'am, but we have a warrant for your son's arrest for failure to appear on a DUI charge," advised Mel in a soft voice. *What a nice guy Mel is,* thought Pete. The woman let the officers into the house, and they went to the room that the woman pointed out. She did not appear to be too upset at the warrant for her son.

As the cops entered the room, they were surprised by the decorations on the walls. Pictures of Yoga and all kinds of posters pertaining to the Hindu religion. Incense was burning on a table in the corner. Not a bad odor compared to most of the places Pete was forced to go to arrest some suspects.

Donald was seated on a large pillow in the middle of the room in the lotus position, with his legs folded up like pretzels. Pete had tried once to get into the lotus position and found it impossible for him. This dude was limber!

"Hey, Swami. We have a warrant for your arrest. Get up," said Pete with his usual crude sense of humor.

"I am meditating and don't want to get up," Donald said in a smooth, quiet voice.

"Ya gotta get up and come with us. Your bail is five hundred dollars."

"But I don't want to. I am trying to have an out-of-body experience," said Donald calmly.

"Look, Swami, if you don't get up and come with us, you gonna have a real out-of-unconsciousness moment soon!" Pete was getting impatient.

After trying to reason with the Swami, Mel and Pete decided to carry Donald to the police vehicle. Donald was small and appeared to weigh about 130 pounds. "Okay, here we go," said Pete and Mel, and they each grabbed a knee and an arm and lifted Donald up.

"Oh, please don't hurt him," pleaded his mother, holding her hand over her heart.

"Don't worry, Mom. He's not in his body right now anyway," quipped Pete as he and Mel struggled toward the long cement steps leading to their car. About halfway up the stairs, it struck Pete that this must really look stupid! Two guys carrying a man who was in the lotus position up a flight of stairs! Pete's back was crying out in pain by the time they reached to top of the stairs and threw Donald into the back seat after putting him in handcuffs. By that time, Donald had returned to his body, and he began to cuss the cops out roundly. Pete's back hurt for several days. Mel thought it was "good exercise!"

Chapter Three

The hallway of the run-down apartment building on Bixel Street was starting to darken as the sun dropped behind the City of Angels skyline. The noise of the traffic rushing by on the Harbor Freeway just a few yards away was ever present. The apartment building was one of three that stood in a row on the west side of Bixel Street, a narrow dirty street that ran downhill from Seventh Street to the entrance of the freeway at the bottom on Eighth Street. The area, once a nice part of downtown Los Angeles, was now almost entirely populated by Latinos, ex-cons and winos.

The door to an apartment on the third floor opened, and a tall Hispanic man in his early thirties stepped out into the hall. As the voice of his wife followed him out the door, he turned and the two exchanged words in Spanish.

"Why do you go out every night and leave me here alone with the kids? You don't work! All you do is drink and fight!" the slightly built Mexican woman complained.

"Shut up, woman! I should send you back to Mexico! And those crying kids too!"

Julio Rivera slammed the door and walked down the stairs to meet his friends, who waited below in the street. As he passed the open door to the apartment of the building manager, he noticed her puttering around inside. Julio didn't like her. She was too strict about the house rules. No visitors after ten at night. No parties. No friends upstairs after ten. Someday he'd fix her.

"*Bruja*," he muttered as he opened the front door and went out into the street.

The apartment manager, Mrs. Cecile Bordeaux, had immigrated to the United States many years ago from Quebec Province in Canada. She still had a strong French Canadian accent. An attractive, petite woman at sixty-three, she took no guff from any of her tenants. She managed all three of the Bixel Street apartment buildings, and their owner was well pleased with her ability to keep order in a business that was difficult and stressful. To her, Julio was just another unruly tenant.

Julio was an illegal alien. Like more than a million others in California, he had entered the United States illegally from Mexico several years before. He had worked for a while but decided it was easier to steal for a living than to work. His specialty was strong-armed street robbery. He did it all the time. He liked to beat people anyway. *Why not get paid for doing it?* he reasoned.

Unlike many of his countrymen, Julio was tall. At a little over six feet, he was several inches taller than the average male of his own country. Julio liked that. It made him feel better and stronger than his peers. Not only tall, the guy was muscular and well built. To add to his formidable appearance, he had the kind of face that made Frankenstein's monster look like Cary Grant. His face was pockmarked and had several scars he had collected from the many fights he has had in the past. Julio was proud of his appearance; he knew it scared the hell out of his victims and made his job easier.

Julio soon discovered that crime paid in California. Especially in Los Angeles, where the cops were few and so overworked, the chances of going to jail for doing his thing on the streets were slim. Busted for drunkenness on the street a couple of times, Julio had never appeared in court on any of the charges. He used phony ID cards, which were easily obtained in downtown Los Angeles, or he just gave a phony name and never showed up in court. He never worried about any of his friends turning him in. They all feared Julio. He was big and they had seen him in action when one of his former partners had threatened to blow the whistle on Julio. The man simply disappeared one day. Because of his criminal activities, several warrants were out on Julio under several different names. Since many of his victims were also illegal aliens, his chances of being reported by them were slim.

Tonight, Julio and his two friends would head down into South Central Los Angeles and rip off a couple of their *hermanos* for some spending cash. Julio could hardly wait to get into action so he could work off the anger and frustration brought on by his complaining wife. Somebody was going to pay. Then he and his *amigos* would celebrate with some *tequila buena*.

"Do you mind if I drive?" asked Mel. "I get carsick when someone else drives."

"Do you mind if I fall asleep?" asked Pete. "I get sleepy when I don't drive." They both laughed. Mel drove. It worked out well because Pete was more familiar with the locations of streets in Los Angeles from years of working traffic all over town. So Pete mapped out their game plan for the day and the routes they would take. Their assigned areas were Seventy-seventh, Newton, and Hollenbeck divisions. The Seventy-seventh Street Division and Newton

Street Division areas were predominantly black and the Hollenbeck Division was mostly Hispanic in population.

Mel was happy when he discovered that Pete spoke pretty good Spanish. Pete had learned it in high school and while working with Mexicans on his previous job in a factory. Many of the people in the game were Hispanics who spoke little or no English. Mel could hardly understand dude jive, let alone Spanish!

The new partners developed strategies on how they would play the game. Their territories comprised some of the toughest parts of town. One of them would go to the front door, while the other would cover the back. Then they would switch.

Dogs were a big concern. Many people kept dogs as protection against theft and trespassing, but dogs don't know the difference between a cop's leg and a burglar's. Mel was a dog lover but not so Pete. Dogs were a pain in the ass to him.

"This should make the *Times News* tomorrow," said Pete as he looked at the next greenie they were going to run on in Newton Division. "It's a warrant for Elizabeth Taylor!"

"Really?" said Mel in honest amazement.

"Yeah. Female Negro, fifty-nine years old, one hundred pounds," read Pete from the warrant's face. "Wanted for petty theft, five hundred dollars bail."

Mel laughed and shook his head as they pulled up in front of the run-down old house on Thirty-ninth Street.

"Elizabeth Taylor," he muttered as they got out of the car. They went around to the back, to the little house in the rear that bore the correct address for Elizabeth Taylor. A dog growled and leapt at the officers, who jumped back, startled. Fortunately, the dog was on a chain that was short enough to keep him away from the cops.

"Mrs. Taylor," said Pete in a loud voice as he knocked on the door.

"Who is it?" asked a little voice inside.

"Police, ma'am," said Mel. "Open the door, please." *Mel was so polite,* thought Pete.

"What choo wont?" she asked in a gruff tone.

"We have a warrant for your arrest, ma'am. Open the door."

"I ain't openin' no do' 'cause you'll arres' me," said the voice.

"If you don't open the door, we'll have to kick it down. You don't want that do you?" asked Pete.

"I'm callin' my lawyer right now," said the voice.

"We're giving you thirty seconds to open the door, and then we're going to have to kick it in," said Pete. They looked at their watches. Inside the house, the woman continued to ramble about her lawyer. Pete looked at Mel.

"It's your turn," he reminded.

Pete and Mel took turns if a door had to be kicked in. Most cops liked kicking doors, even though it could be dangerous. It was like in the movies. Except movie cops use their shoulder to do it. Pete knew of no one who had ever knocked down a door that way in real life. One could easily break a shoulder. Cops are taught to kick the part of the door near the lock, close to the doorjamb.

"Hmm," mumbled Mel. His first kick rattled the door and *shook the whole wall!* The second kick told the cops that the entire wall of the house might cave in!

"Whoa! Stop! I can see the headlines now," Pete predicted. "LAPD Destroys Elderly Black Woman's Home for Petty Theft Arrest! God help us." Mel kicked again and the door gave way. The cops went in.

Elizabeth Taylor stood before them in all her beauty. She was skinny and shriveled up, wearing only a sheer nightgown, which showed all her feminine attributes. With the phone in one hand, she waved her skinny finger at the cops with the other.

"My lawyer be on the phone right now," she warned.

"Well, let me talk to him," said Pete as he took the receiver from her. "Hello?" To his surprise there *was* someone on the other end!

"This is Officer Felix, LAPD. We're arresting Mrs. Taylor on a bench warrant." He went on to explain how she could be bailed out. After he hung up, he turned to Mrs. Taylor. "Ma'am, you'll have to get dressed and come with us."

"How I goin' change my clothes wit you pol-lice in my room?"

"We'll step out into the other room, but we have to leave the door open, in case you try to escape," said Mel in his gentleman's tone.

"I ain' tryin' to 'scape. You white boys jus' want to see my nekkid."

"No, ma'am, I guarantee you we don't!" said Pete as he turned his back on the open door. She kept up a steady stream of comments from the other room. After about two minutes, she stepped back into the living room and confronted Pete and his partner.

"An' another thing," said Liz. This time she only had on nothing but a pair of bright red panties! Pete cringed as he saw her two dark brown breasts like half-empty water balloons hanging down nearly to her navel.

"You got no right to break down my do'," she yelled, waving her arms around wildly, which caused the two hanging body parts to wobble back and forth like wilted lilies in the wind. *Oh god*, thought Pete, *I hope we survive this.*

They booked her and later had fun telling the guys in the unit about the arrest and the booking of Elizabeth Taylor. Of course, they built up the story until the last minute when they had to describe *their* Elizabeth Taylor!

Chapter Four

"How's the new job going?" asked Noel as Pete attempted to tie a Windsor knot in his tie. *Why can't I ever tie it right the first time?* he thought to himself as he struggled.

"The job is doing fine. I don't know how good I'm doing at it." He finished the touches on his tie and strapped on his Smith & Wesson .38 revolver. Since his transfer from uniformed duty to a plainclothes job, Pete had stopped carrying his old S&W with the four-inch barrel that was required when working in uniform. *Too big, if you don't have to carry it,* he thought. Now he was allowed to carry a smaller pistol. He had purchased a used pistol with a two-inch barrel, which was less bulky to carry in plain clothes. Instead of the smaller, five-shot model, he bought the six-shot version. It was a little heavier, but he liked the comfort of the additional round. It still had to be only a .38 caliber, however.

"How're you and your new partner getting along?" she asked.

"We're doing fine. Mel's really a nice guy. Maybe too nice to be a cop. I worry that someday someone will nail him because he's a little too nice to people." Pete had known several cops who were now pushing up the sod in Forest Lawn Cemetery because they were "too nice" and got their asses shot off. There was a middle ground where a cop could maintain a friendly attitude with people but still protect himself. In the more than eighteen years Pete had been a cop, he had never been injured by a suspect. He'd been hurt in fights and accidents, but never had he allowed a suspect to "cop a Sunday punch on him," as the cops called it. He intended to keep that record going.

When Pete arrived at work that day, he remembered that Mel had taken the day off and he was working with Bobby Gomez. Gomez seemed to be a good cop, although Pete thought of him as just the opposite of Mel. Gomez was a little too hard on people.

"Hey, Bobby," greeted Pete, "it's you and me today. Whose area do you want to work, yours or mine?"

Bobby was a well-built ex-marine who had done his time in Vietnam. He had been in the military about seven years before coming on the job. In his mid-thirties, Bobby had black hair and, although he had a name that was Hispanic and looked like he was, he said he was not. The fact was he really didn't know; since he had been an adopted child, no information seemed to exist for him about his biological parents. He didn't seem to care about it. Pete liked him in spite of his gruff exterior.

As Bobby and Pete headed out for the south end of town, they chatted.

"How come you left motors, man? I thought you guys got a pay bonus for riding those murder cycles," said Bobby as he drove.

"We did but I discovered there *is* life after motors. It just got to be a pain in the ass. The supervisors pressure you for more tickets, and at the same time they want you to take accident reports and do everything else the other cops in patrol cars do. Motors used to be a specialized job enforcing traffic laws. Now, since they decentralized the squad and put the motor cops under the supervision of the patrol divisions, it's a new ball game. It wasn't fun anymore." Pete actually missed the motor squad and wished he could go back, but he knew it wouldn't be the same. Anyway, he really hadn't given this job a good try yet.

Bobby had been in the warrant unit for about a year before Pete joined it, and Pete still had questions.

"I'm still kind of new around here, Bobby. Why the big deal in court about *due diligence* on warrants?"

"Well, when a warrant is issued by the court, someone has to try to serve it. If more than a year goes by without a documented attempt, it can be thrown out of court. You see, some court has ruled that police agencies must use *due diligence* in attempting to serve a warrant. In other words, try to find the asshole and bust him on the warrant. I guess they figure if we don't care, why should the court?" That seemed to make sense to Pete.

"Yeah, I remember that. Then why don't we have a bunch of cops out looking for these assholes?"

"Most people think it's more important to catch criminals while they're committing the crimes. Once we put 'em in jail and they're convicted or fined, people think it's all over and they forget about it. So J. Willy Roundass decides to jump bail or not show up in court and a warrant is issued for him. He buries himself in this haystack we call the city and becomes a needle we need to find. He can avoid us for years sometimes. He usually gets caught when one of your motor cop buddies stops him for a ticket and runs a warrant check on him. Now that wants and warrants are in a computer, we can dig out the want in a hurry."

"How many warrants do you think we have in the files?" asked Pete, realizing it was a dumb question as soon as he asked it.

"Millions," said Bobby. "We don't even worry about traffic or parking tickets! We only go after what we call 'high-grade misdemeanors' in our unit."

"I didn't realize things were that bad."

"Once in a while, they'll run a computer check on just parking ticket warrants alone and find a few dorks that just don't feel they're required to pay their fines. Some of them have run up thousands of dollars worth of warrants, and we'll go after those deadbeats as well. I had a guy one time who owed several thousand dollars in parking warrants. Actually, we're out here shoveling shit against the tide," said Bobby.

"But that's what we do all the time anyway, isn't it?"

"Yeah, our main job out here is to perform the 'diligence' part of the warrants to keep them alive. It's hard not to want to book all the assholes that have warrants. The good thing is when we catch 'em, we *have* to book 'em because it's a command on the warrant. No Miranda Rights and no arrest reports. Then, if an arrested person challenges the validity of the warrant, we are considered an expert witness as a *custodian of records* and can testify if a warrant has had a due diligence attempt at being served."

"Great!" said Pete. "Let's obey the courts!"

They pulled up in front of a neat house in south central Los Angeles, in what the media calls "The Ghetto." Of course, most cops think there is no ghetto in Los Angeles and never was but the derogatory term serves the needs of the politicians, so it exists.

Pete read from the greenie, "This chick is wanted for prostitution. Bail is five hundred dollars. Female. Black. She's five feet two, black and brown, 105 pounds. DOB of 1/12/52."

The officers knocked on the front door, making sure not to stand directly in front of it just in case someone wanted to shoot a couple of cops through the door. As the door opened, the cops had their ID cards in their hands.

"Police, ma'am. Are you Virginia Worthington?" asked Bobby. The black woman was skinny and not very attractive. A quick look told the cops that she was very close to the physical description on the warrant.

"No. I ain't Virginia. What choo want her fo'," she said with a frown and a growling voice.

"We have a warrant for her arrest. What's your name?" asked Pete. He caught the usual slight hesitation while the person being questioned desperately tries to think of a good lie.

"My name Louise. Virginia my sister," she said.

"Would you show us your identification, please," Bobby asked.

"I don' have no ID. This is my house! I don' need no ID to be in my own house!" she yelled.

"What's your birth date?" asked Pete as he pointed his finger in the woman's face to put pressure on her answer.

"Uh. January 12, 1952," she blurted out.

"Gee whiz," said Pete in an overly concerned voice, "That's the same day your sister was born!"

"Uh . . . uh, we be twins," she stammered.

"Buzzzzt!" sounded Pete. "Wrong answer! You be's Virginia."

"No, I ain't! I done tol' you! She my sister!"

"Well, you're goin' to jail for your sister then," advised Bobby. "Now get some clothes on, and let's go." The woman was wearing a housecoat over a night gown.

"I has to change in my room," she said in a sharp, irritated voice, and she quickly went into the bed room and slammed the door.

"You do that," said Pete. Bobby looked at Pete as the woman closed the only door to the bedroom. The back door of the house was right next to the bedroom door. Pete counted out loud.

"One, two, three, four . . ." When he got to ten, he opened the back door and stood beneath the bedroom window. As the woman came jumping out, now fully clothed, she fell into the waiting arms of the cops. After a brief struggle, the handcuffs were on and she was on her way to jail.

"Where's your partner today, Petey?" asked Billy Much. The guys were sitting around their respective tables sorting out greenies for the day's game. Pete had been in the unit about six months now and was fairly well acquainted with the unit's functions.

"Melvin's off today," said Pete. "I'm going out alone today. And don't call me Petey, asshole!"

The officers of the Warrant Unit were not prohibited from working alone, as long as they didn't get themselves into trouble trying to put people in jail. When working without a partner, mostly they just performed "due diligence" by hanging warrant notices on the doors or giving them to the occupants of addresses listed on warrants. This satisfied the minimum diligence required for keeping the warrant "alive."

Pete checked out an unmarked police car and headed for some of his old stomping grounds when he worked Central Division Patrol years ago as a rookie. He had picked out some warrants in the Silver Lake District of what was now Rampart Division. In the old days, it had been his 1A1 patrol beat in Central Division. The boundaries had since changed.

So had the territory! The area that had once been an affluent neighborhood with some old-time movie stars as residents had now deteriorated into a dope-infested habitation of lower-class individuals and foreigners. The once beautiful Silver Lake Reservoir was now surrounded by rapidly declining living quarters. Most of the older residents had moved out. Still, driving around the area brought back some fond memories of his first days as a cop in Los Angeles.

He also recalled some of his first days walking a foot beat in downtown Los Angeles in the area just south of where he was now called MacArthur Park. The park was named after the famous World War II general of the same name. There was a nice lake in the middle and lots of people congregated there and there was usually some trouble every day on the streets surrounding the park. Pete reminisced on how the department had changed since he walked his first foot beat. If you were assigned to walk the beat by yourself on the day watch, you were literally out there on your own!

Those were the days before the officers had hand-held radios with which to request help or to call a radio car to transport any arrestee he might have in tow. The closest direct wires to the police station were contained in "call boxes" on the corners every few blocks. They were called the "Gamewell" because that was the name of the company who made them. Each officer was issued a large brass Gamewell key that opened the call box and was to be carried on the officer's belt.

Pete recalled many times when he had wished there was a Gamewell on every corner! Officers soon learned that the best protection for him was to make friends with the local business owners on his beat. There were many times when a beat officer had been saved by a friendly shopkeeper or bartender who called in for help for the officer. But it also bred opportunities for officers to get too friendly with locals that could end up with violations of taking gratuities from them in return for protection. Pete had always shunned most of that stuff, except for and cigar or two now and then.

The main thing he remembered of his first day alone on a foot beat was the feeling of insecurity and the need to stay alert and not be surprised by anything that could endanger his life. There were times when he had to fight a resisting person hand to hand. Most of the time Pete was outweighed by his opponents but was able to defend himself relying on the boxing experience he had gained several years prior to coming on the department. He had participated in the boxing tournaments of the Golden Gloves for two years and had gained a lot of boxing skill that came in handy on the tough beats of Los Angeles. Pete had counted himself lucky to have survived those days without major injuries.

"Any rampart unit in the vicinity," the police radio announced, "a 459 there now at 2235 Teviot Way. Any unit handling, come in." Startled from his reverie, Pete realized he was a few blocks from where the burglary was going down and would probably be the closest unit. As a warrant unit officer, he could not handle the call, but he could back up the officers who were responding. None responded. The radio advised that Air One, the police helicopter unit, was overhead at the location. That was enough for Pete.

"Shop number 347 is going code 6 at 2235 Teviot Way in plain clothes. Air One meet me on Tac two frequency," Pete said into the microphone. When Air One rogered his request, he switched to the tactical frequency. "Air One, this is shop 347. I'm pulling up on front of the address in a white Rambler four-door. Do you see me?" he asked.

"We got you. Do you see anything at the front?" Pete pulled up and stopped in front of the house. It was a small but nice house set back from the street and down the hill about thirty feet. The front door was in sight and appeared to be intact. There were no vehicles in front.

"Negative," said Pete. "Nothing shakin' from here."

"Two male suspects just exited the rear of the house and are running down the hill," said Air One. *The chopper overhead must have spooked the burglars,* thought Pete.

At the same time, a two-man black-and-white Rampart unit that had apparently taken the call drove up.

"They just went out the back," yelled Pete to the newly arriving uniformed officers. They all piled out of their cars and headed for the house. The uniformed officers had hand-held radios and could communicate away from their car. Pete tagged along as backup, not knowing what to expect in the house.

The suspects had too good of a head start and got away. The officers entered the house and could see immediately that the place had been burglarized. Otherwise, the house was empty.

During their ransacking, the intruders had brutally killed a small dog in the house, probably to keep it from barking. After checking the house and the grounds, the uniformed officers were trying to contact the owner of the house in order to secure the property and to make the report. Pete stood outside and chatted with one of the officers. Just then, an old panel truck drove up and a young man stuck his head out of the driver's window.

"You guys looking for somebody? I picked this guy up thumbing a ride a couple of blocks from here. It looked like he was running away. He had grass all over him, and I saw the police helicopter circling above," said the young driver.

The officers looked at each other in amazement. *This guy just happens along and sees a suspicious looking man hitchhiking on the street, sees the police helicopter, and puts two and two together. Then he picks the guy up and brings him back to us,* thought Pete! What a hero! The suspect was taken into custody and handcuffed and placed in the right front seat of the black-and-white.

While one of the officers sat behind the wheel and was filling out the crime report, Pete stood beside the police car and chatted with the "hero" and the other officer. They were both still awed by the realization that this was an ordinary citizen who had the guts to collect one of the suspects and deliver him to the cops.

The "hero" interrupted Pete, asking incredulously, "Are you telling me that this son of a bitch killed a little dog inside the house? Is that right?" asked the hero.

"Yep," answered Pete. Without hesitating a second, the hero tapped on the window of the police car on the passenger's side. The cop inside reached over and rolled the window down. The hero then smacked the suspect on the side of the head with his fist! The man in handcuffs fell over in his seat, stunned. The cop in the car shook his head and calmly rolled the window back up.

"Well, I guess you guys are going to arrest me for hitting that guy now," said the hero with resignation in his voice.

"I didn't see anything. Did you, Officer?" Pete asked the other uniformed officer standing nearby.

"I don't know what you're talking about," said the cop with a serious face. "I think you can go now," he said to the hero. Pete thought it was also time to leave, so he did too.

Chapter Five

"I like dogs, but I hate 'em too!" whined Pete as Mel and he were heading out for the day's game of hide-and-seek. Dogs were everywhere it seemed to Pete. "I don't blame folks for having one to protect their house while they are gone, but it sure makes our job a lot harder."

"I love little puppies," said Mel, mimicking a sweet little kid voice.

"So do I," quipped Pete. "With the proper amount of salsa, they taste great in tacos." Mel frowned at Pete but knew he was only trying to agitate him.

"It's not the 'little puppies' I worry about. It's the *big* puppies! Think of how many assholes don't get arrested because they have a big, vicious dog in the yard? None of the guys I've ever worked with will go into a yard on a minor bust with a big dog in it," complained Pete.

Mel had been wanting to visit the downtown LA dog pound to see if he could find a dog he wanted. He already had two dogs at home. Today, the two partners went to the animal regulation pound on Ann Street to look for a sweet little puppy for Melvin.

"I like little puppies," said Mel, again using his sickening sweet little voice, as the two hardened LAPD cops approached the front door of the pound.

"Me too. If they're here!" While Mel went from cage to cage, looking at dogs, Pete used the opportunity to question the attendant about dog control.

"Tell me something, what's the best way for me to protect against a dog attack?" asked Pete in a serious manner.

"Well, most dogs will bark a lot while you're outside their fence. Once you show them you're not afraid and go inside their fence, they usually back down. But never turn your back on them or they'll get ya," lectured the attendant in an official sounding tone. He seemed flattered that a cop would ask his advice. He continued, "Most dogs are cowards when challenged. Only trained dogs will attack, although you never really know," he said.

"What could I do to allow me to get into yards where a dog is on duty?" asked Pete. In the background, Mel was coochie cooing a little puppy in one of the cages. Pete tried to ignore him.

"If you're attacked by a dog and you have nothing to defend with, bend down and pretend you're picking up a rock and are going to throw it. That'll make 'em think. If you see a stick, use it. Or even a rolled up newspaper. Dogs are afraid of things that look like weapons in your hand. Of course, if he's trained to attack, you might as well shoot the son of a bitch."

"I really appreciate your advice," said Pete. "Thanks a lot."

"You're welcome."

"Well, Mel. Have you kissed any of the little puppies or seen any females you want to mate with?" asked Pete. Mel stuck his tongue out at his partner.

"I've got an idea," said Pete as they walked back to their car.

"You're going to get a puppy?" asked Mel in the voice.

"No, Fido. I'm going to get a stick. The police batons we carry are twenty-six inches long. Too long to carry in plain clothes. It would look too . . . combative. I'm going to cut mine off so that it fits up my sleeve to about the elbow. I can hold it up there with my hand and no one would see it. If I needed it, I just straighten my arm and let it slide out into my hand. Bingo!"

"Sounds dumb to me," said Mel.

"You want to kiss dogs and you call me dumb?" teased Pete. "You've been spending too much time on those hard, narrow bicycle seats, Partner."

"But I like little puppies," said Melvin.

That night at home, Pete cut his baton down to a length that when held in the palm of his hand, would fit inside his coat or shirtsleeve up to the elbow, still allowing the arm to bend. It worked great! He put it in his gear bag and took it to work. The next time they went out on the hunt, he took it along.

They were working in the Highland Park Division, in the hills of Mt. Washington, and came to a house with a chain-link fence around it. As the guys walked up to the gate, they saw the sign that said Beware of Dog, but no canine was in sight. The officers had learned to estimate the size of a dog by looking for dog crap in a yard. Big crap equals big dog. Little crap, little dog. Pretty simple.

"Big *caca*," warned Mel. "I wonder where the pooch is." Pete stopped and went back to the car for his "batonette." Pete rattled the gate, and they found out. He came from the backyard with a roar. The huge black Doberman ran up to the gate, barking, growling, and snapping viciously at the two cops.

"After you," said Melvin, bowing, waving his hand. Pete looked at his partner with a scared grin that expressed his desire not to really have to test his dog-protection theory.

"I like puppies," said Pete, imitating Mel's little voice. "Well, there's only one way to test the guy's theory," he said, sliding the little baton into his hand and opening the gate.

As the gate swung open, Pete pointed the baton directly at the growling monster. "You aren't going to eat me now, are you, Puppy?" Pete said, holding the baton like a gun pointed at the dog.

It was like magic! The dog stopped barking and growling and backed up toward the front porch. Pete advanced on the animal with Mel behind, his hand on his gun. The dog continued to retreat until he was peeking at the cops from around the corner of the house. Mel went to the door and knocked while Pete stood guard on their rear.

The Hispanic lady who opened the door was startled when she saw the officers in her yard. Apparently no one had ever gotten that far before without being eaten alive. "Where's my dog?" she asked.

"Oh, he's right over there," said Pete, pointing to the cowering beast. "The Los Angeles Police Department likes little puppies," advised Pete. The dog had a whipped look on his face.

Dogs were seldom a problem after that, but there was an occasional exception. A few days after the first dog encounter, the two cops arrived at an address on a warrant. There was a small white dog in the yard. Pete pulled out his "dog discourager," went through the gate, and got a surprise: The little dog came rushing to attack. Pete yelled at the beast, pointed the baton at it, and got another surprise: Apparently Pete's magic weapon didn't discourage *this* little doggie. Pete literally pushed the baton in the dog's face in an attempt to ward off the attack. The little dog chomped down on his baton like an ear of corn!

Later, after the owner saved the life of the dog, Pete looked at his baton. "Damn, Mel! Look at all the teeth marks that little bastard made on my baton!"

"Well, he was a nice little dog doing his best to protect his home," Mel advised.

"Okay, but it's a good thing those teeth marks weren't on my leg or he wouldn't need a home!"

"You are so bad!" Mel ended the conversation.

"Hey, Petey," said Billy Much in his usual loud and obnoxious voice. "How about working with me today in Seventy-seventh?" Pete had worked with Billy a couple of times before, and in some ways, Billy reminded him of Uncle Ed. Not just because he smoked but also because of his attitude toward work. It was similar to Ed's. He didn't like to do too much, contrary to his name. But he was fun to be around and had a good sense of humor so Pete agreed.

"Don't call me Petey, asshole!"

"You drive, okay, Pete?" Billy knew that Pete was more familiar with the territory, and besides, then, he could smoke and kick back. They checked out the car and headed out.

"How come you always listen to the damned radio?" asked Much.

"Wouldn't you feel bad if some cop got killed and we were only a block away?" Pete said.

"Naw," said Billy. "Fuck 'em. They oughta get out of patrol anyway."

"Somebody's got to do it. Okay, you can just sit in the car and smoke, and I'll do the work, *Uncle Ed*," chided Pete.

"Thanks a lot," grumbled Billy, indicating his displeasure at being compared to Uncle Ed.

They made several uneventful stops for due diligence before coming to the house on Lou Dillon Avenue in Watts. The house was one of the most run down on the block. The warrant was for a male Negro for violation of probation on a drug matter. The cops got out of the car and, as they approached the house, noticed that the side door to the driveway was open. When a door of a house is standing open, officers usually announce themselves and walk in.

"Police officers," called Pete as he hesitated at the open door. No answer. They could hear the sound of a TV set from inside the house. Pete called again a little louder, "Police officers. We're coming in!"

As they stepped into the kitchen area, the startled roaches on the floor ran in herds, trying to get away! There were empty food cans and bottles littering the floor. Food was rotting on the stove, and the sink was full of dirty dishes covered with slime.

"Jesus Christ," moaned Billy as the stench hit their noses, causing the two veteran cops to stop in their tracks! They proceeded cautiously into the interior of the house. In the "living room," if it could be called that, were two little black kids sitting on a filthy torn-up couch. They were both under five years old, dressed in filthy clothes and wore no shoes. It was impossible to tell if they were girls, boys, or one of each. The kids were watching a TV set whose picture was barely discernible, full of snow and with lines going up and down the tube.

"Where's your mama and daddy?" asked Pete. The little kids just looked at him as if they didn't understand English. Pete tried Spanish. *"Donde esta' su mama y papa?"* he asked. No response.

"We need to call for a Juvie car here, Partner," said Pete. It didn't take a second for Billy to catch on.

"I'll do it! You stay here." Billy hurriedly left for the police car, lighting up a cigarette as he ran. The Juvenile Division unit showed up in about a half hour. Neither Pete nor Billy could stand the smell inside the house so they waited on the side porch. Billy didn't stop smoking and even the cigarette smoke smelled good to Pete compared to the inside of that house. The kids were taken into custody for their safety. The parents never showed up. A neighbor said she would tell them where their kids were. The Juvie officers left a business card. It was close to end of watch as Pete and Billy drove back to the station. They tried to talk out their feelings.

"That's the worst home I've ever been in," said Pete, "and I've worked all over this fucking town!" He was mad!

So was Billy, but he wasn't responsive. He just smoked and said, "No shit!"

"I wish every person who used dope, any kind of dope, could see what the results of addiction can be. I wish all those bleeding-heart assholes who live in Beverly Hills and defend dopers and vote for all these liberal bastards who want to make drugs legal had to live in that house for a week!" Pete yelled. "I wish . . ." He paused, knowing most wishes don't come true. "Fuck 'em all!" he muttered as a final statement. They drove the rest of the way to the station in silence.

Mel parked in front of the four-story apartment building on Bixel between Seventh and Eighth. "This is the address," said Pete as he stuffed the warrant abstract in his pocket.

Pete remembered this street well. Several years ago, he and another motor cop had been returning from a VIP motorcycle escort detail in the rain. When they got to Seventh and Bixel, it had started to drizzle rain. Walt, Pete's partner, had just turned right at the corner ahead of him to ride down the Bixel Hill to the freeway. Walt's bike lost traction on the slippery pavement and went down on its right side. Walt was unhurt and the motorcycle was not damaged due to the slow speed of the turn. Pete had stopped to help Walt pick up his motor and was laughing at his partner for falling down. The pavement had been so slippery that as Pete walked out into the street to help, his boots "lost traction" and he literally skied all the way to the bottom of the hill on his feet! Then it was his partner's turn to laugh at Pete! Shit, he missed those days.

"What's this guy wanted for?" asked Mel, breaking up Pete's memories of earlier times.

"Uh . . . oh, no big deal. Just a DUI," mumbled Pete. They climbed the five or six steps to the door of the apartment building. It looked to Pete like a thousand other buildings he'd been in during his career. Musty smelling, with creaky old elevators. Those that had elevators that is. Once inside the building, Pete was surprised at the cleanliness of this building. It even looked neat! The sign said Manager over the first apartment on the left. Pete knocked.

Mrs. Bordeaux came to the door. "What ees eet?" she asked in her French Canadian accent. At first sight, Pete thought how pale she was. Her hair was either very blond or very white or a combination of both. She was neatly dressed, and her blue eyes had a glint of mischievousness. Pete guessed she was in her early sixties. Pete thought she was rather attractive.

"Hi, I'm Officer Felix, and this is Officer Tennesen. Are you the manager?"

"Yais, I am zee manager. What ees wrong?"

"We have a warrant for the arrest of Jose Barranca. He gave this address and apartment 209."

"Oh, he ees move away long time ago. I throw heem out! That apartment ees vacant now."

"Well, do you mind if we take a look?" asked Mel.

"You theenk I lie to you, eh?" teased the old woman. "Come. I show you."

The cops followed her up the stairway leading to the second floor. An unusually large Hispanic man was coming down the stairs as they were going up, and they moved aside to let him pass. He glowered at the two cops as they passed without speaking.

"Why don' you arrest that one, eh? Ee's no good. Beat his wife. Drink. Fight! Someday I throw eem out too!" The manager then started speaking in French, but her meaning was clear. She did not like her tenant.

She showed the cops the vacant room and was very cooperative. She went on to praise the police for keeping the streets safe. Pete wondered what streets she was talking about. She couldn't mean the streets near here! They were teeming with vermin and bad guys!

They finished their work at that address and left. Mel and Pete were to see Mrs. Bordeaux fairly often in the course of looking for suspects in that area of Los Angeles. They learned that she managed not only that building but the two other four-story apartment buildings in that block on Bixel Street. All of the buildings were owned by the Cadillac car agency on the corner of Seventh and Bixel. Mrs. Bordeaux was always cheerful and cooperative and complimentary, and Pete liked her spunkiness.

Chapter Six

Pete rode his own private motorcycle to work nowadays. It was easier on gas, and there were fewer of the parking problems that the other cops had. Privately owned motorcycles were allowed to park in the triangular spaces at the end of the aisles of the police vehicle parking, located under the police building parking lot.

"You're still riding those murder-cycles, huh?" asked D. J. Willis as they met walking into the police building from the parking area. "As I recall, you had one when we were working Central almost twenty years ago. Then you rode motors on the job for a long time, and now you're still ridin' 'em?"

Pete liked the older black officer with the graying hair. He had always been a nice person and a good partner to work with.

"Yeah, I can't seem to get it out of my blood. I've only been without a motorcycle to ride for about three years since 1958, and those were three miserable years. It's easy to find a parking spot. You can zip through traffic, *and* it's fun!" said Pete embellishing on the last part of his statement.

"Doesn't it scare you when you go between the lanes on the freeway like that?"

"Naw, you can do it safely if you keep your speed under control and watch out for lane changers. If they ever make it illegal to split lanes in California, I'll be screwed. And so will the cops because that's one of the advantages of riding a police motorcycle: you can get through traffic." They entered the back door of the police building and headed for R&I on the mezzanine floor.

It turned out to be one of those boring "due diligence" days for Pete and Mel. A long day but definitely routine.

As Pete headed for the parking area, where his Italian-built Moto Guzzi motorcycle was parked, he was looking forward to the ride home. He had been riding a Moto Guzzi police motorcycle on duty and had been impressed with the smooth way the vehicle handled. He bought a used Moto Guzzi bike to ride back and forth to work. The bike was black with white pin striping, of the same model and year he had been riding on the job. The bike was his "baby."

The dull workday was history. Pete was on his bike and headed toward the Pomona Freeway and home. Threading his way through the late-afternoon freeway traffic on the Pomona Freeway, he passed between lanes one and two. As he rode, he thought how frustrating it is to drive a car in Los Angeles' traffic and wondered why more people didn't ride motorcycles or scooters. Using the skills he had gained from being a motor cop for more than fifteen years, he gracefully worked his way through the bogged-down traffic toward home and a cold beer.

As he passed between lanes one and two on the Pomona Freeway, he saw the quick movement of a car out of the corner of his left eye. He instantly accelerated and moved to his right. The Chevy's swerve toward him had been abrupt and must almost certainly have been intentional. Pete thought it was an attempt to scare him as he passed by. In any event, he was certain it was a movement made with intent.

Pete pulled into the lane to his right and ahead of the Chevy, away from danger. Then he looked back over his shoulder and saw the driver. The man was about thirty-five or maybe a little younger. It was hard to tell because of his full beard and long hair. He was laughing and pointing at Pete! His passenger was a younger man and clean-shaven. He was also laughing at the "big joke" the driver had played in scaring the motorcycle rider. Pete understood why some motorists didn't like motorcycles and why some of them honked and cursed at them when they infiltrated traffic on the freeways. But the motorcyclists were doing nothing illegal, so it was usually a case of ignorance on the part of the car driver.

Pete felt anger rise in his chest when he saw the car driver laughing. *Doesn't he realize what he's doing could have caused me to have an accident?* he thought. Pete nodded his head at the Chevy's driver and gave him a thumbs-up with his left hand, as if to say, "Nice going, pal." Then he accelerated to get away from the idiot. The incident was almost forgotten after a couple of miles.

Then Pete noticed the men in the Chevy again in his rearview mirror. They were working their way through traffic to catch up with him. Warning bells started going off in his cop brain. The Chevy got in behind him as Pete rode in the far right lane. The car pulled up dangerously close behind Pete's rear wheel. Pete turned and glared at the driver. He was laughing again.

Being threatened by a two-thousand-pound chunk of metal called a car is not a pleasant thing when you're riding a motorcycle. Pete moved to his left and out of the path of the Chevy. The car pulled alongside his motorcycle. The driver's window was down.

"What's the matter with you? Are you crazy?" Pete yelled at the driver. The driver of the Chevy answered by swerving to his left and crashing into Pete's motorcycle! The impact sent the bike swerving into the next lane to the left. Fortunately there was a space there for his bike to occupy. If he'd gone down in this traffic, it would have been all over for Pete and he knew it!

That's it, Pete thought to himself. *This has gone far enough!* Pete reached into his hip pocket and pulled out his badge holder. He moved back alongside the Chevy and held out the badge and yelled, "I'm a police officer. Pull over. You're under arrest!"

The Chevy swerved again to its left. This time Pete was ready for it. He swerved left with the Chevy. The impact of the car hitting the bike was minimal, but again there was contact. Pete dropped back and made some big decisions. What was happening right now was a felonious assault with a deadly weapon on a police officer. A car can be as deadly a weapon as any other. Even more in this case. Pete reached into his belt and pulled his two-inch barreled .38 revolver. Games were over now! He planned his next move.

If the driver tried to hit him again, Pete could lawfully shoot him in self-defense. *But*, he thought, *with my luck, I'd miss that guy and hit the poor guy sitting next to him, who probably isn't guilty of anything but a poor choice of friends. If I do hit the driver, he may then go out of control and hit me or some other vehicle. No, shooting this jerk is out no matter what, but he has to be apprehended.* Pete decided to shoot out one of the Chevy's tires, force the guy to stop, and then arrest him. Although the confrontation had been going on now for about seven or eight miles, Pete had not noticed that the traffic behind the two vehicles had slowed to watch the conflict.

Traffic ahead was starting to thin out as they approached the 605 Freeway. Pete again pulled alongside the Chevy, this time with gun in hand.

Again he yelled, "Police! Pull over!" Now the bearded driver accelerated rapidly, trying to get away. Pete pulled up, and at close range, fired a round into the left rear tire. Nothing! *I couldn't have missed*, he thought. *In the movies, the car tires always blow out when shot!* he thought.

By this time, the Chevy was traveling at a high rate of speed. Pete stayed with the car at a safe distance behind. He finally noticed that all the traffic behind was hanging back. Of course, they were. They'd been watching the whole thing for miles!

The Chevy started to pull over. *Finally*, thought Pete as he saw the tire going flat. It only took a few miles! *Movies suck*, he thought. As the Chevy pulled onto the shoulder, Pete saw another car pulling over behind him. The driver was signaling thumbs up. *A friend*, thought Pete. *And I need one now!* Pete got off his motorcycle and showed his badge to the driver of the other car that had stopped to help. The guy nodded. Then Pete turned to the Chevy. The bearded driver was getting out, and so was the passenger.

"Police! Both of you, down on the ground, face down," Pete yelled and covered the pair with his gun. The passenger immediately went down on his face. The bearded driver did not comply. Instead, he moved to the front of the car. Pete covered him and approached cautiously. The suspect didn't drop to the ground, nor did he put his hands up in surrender. Again Pete yelled, "I said get down on the ground *now!*" The man again refused to comply.

By this time, Pete was within a few feet of the belligerent man. The guy was big and burly. By his appearance, Pete pegged him as the type you encounter in bars who try to throw their weight around and bully people. Pete had run into this kind many times before. They don't give up easily. Their egos won't let them.

"I'm calling the Highway Patrol," said the bearded man. He was close to a freeway call box attached to a light pole a few feet away. Pete knew he had to get control *fast!*

"The Highway Patrol is on the way right now," said Pete. "Now get down on the ground. I told you you're under arrest!" The man faced Pete in defiance. It's now or never, Pete knew. He reached out with his left hand to grab the suspect, knowing he would not allow Pete to grab him. When the suspect reached for Pete's hand, Pete brought the Smith & Wesson down on the guy's head as hard as he could! The man staggered back but did not go down! *I hate movies*, thought Pete as scenes of people falling when hit with pistols in movies flashed before him.

Now they were down on the ground together, rolling around, the man grappling for Pete's gun. This was now a deadly game. Now Pete was on top of the man. With a wrenching movement that took all his strength, Pete freed his gun-hand and shoved the gun barrel hard into one of the man's nostrils.

"This is it, asshole!" yelled Pete as he put pressure on the trigger.

"Okay, okay!" yelled the man. "I give up!" He relaxed his struggle and lay still.

Pete stood up and yelled at the Good Samaritan who had stopped to help.

"In my right saddle bag, there is a pair of handcuffs. Would you bring them here?" All the fight had gone out of the suspect as he sat leaning against the pole, bleeding from the large laceration Pete's pistol had made on his obviously empty head!

The Highway Patrol did show up shortly, as well as an LA motor cop on his way home. The bearded man went to jail charged with assault with a deadly weapon. The passenger went also went to jail on outstanding traffic warrants. His game of hide-and-seek was over. Trial dates were set for later. The LAPD's shooting review board ruled that Pete's use of his pistol was justified. Generally, LAPD cops are not supposed to shoot at moving vehicles, but since he was being assaulted, it was justified. Pete looked forward to the trial and sending this guy to prison.

Chapter Seven

Shuffling through a pile of warrants every day can be boring, but it's part of the job. The new warrants that come in daily must be sorted into the divisions where suspects' addresses are located and then into piles according to the reporting district within that division. Each officer or team does this job in the morning before they leave to play the warrant game.

Pete was sorting new warrants this morning while Mel was on the phone, calling suspects where the officers had left notices on previous attempts to serve a warrant. After leaving a notice on a door, if the cops have time, they may look up the suspect's phone number in the phone book or the "Backward Phone Book." The Backward Book lists phone numbers by address instead of by name. It is only available to law enforcement agencies on request. It came in handy on many occasions.

"Hey," said Pete, "I know this chick." He stared at the abstract of the warrant in the name of Sherry Barone, with an address in Highland Park. Memories came pouring back as if a dam had broken in his head.

"Who is it?" asked his partner. Pete looked around the room. Several guys were listening.

"Tell ya later." After leaving the office, Pete and Mel headed for their favorite breakfast stop, the LAPD Academy restaurant. Pete loved the sausage and the eggs and the onions they put in the hashed browned potatoes. The old academy also brought back happy memories, and he could relax there.

"Sherry Barone is the daughter of Evie Barone, an old girl friend of mine. Evie and I had a hot love affair about fifteen years ago, when I was a new kid on the motor squad." Pete's thoughts ran back to the good times that he and Evie had enjoyed together riding motorcycles. The trip they took to Seattle to the World's Fair in 1962. The great view of Green Lake they had from the apartment they had rented for the week. The laughs and the fun they enjoyed together. He told Mel the whole story while they ate.

He revealed how, after falling in love with Evie, he discovered she was apparently two different personalities. The one he knew and loved was not the same one who, according to police records Pete later found, gave her ten-year-old daughter marijuana and sold it to other kids in her neighborhood! He had also discovered that she had some shady friends Pete knew nothing about.

"I broke up with her soon after that. You know how 'the department' feels about cops in those kinds of relationships." Mel nodded in agreement.

"About a year later, I ran into Evie again as she was being brought into the Central Detectives for questioning on a 211. Her car had been used in a robbery of the Pioneer Market on Sunset. She swore she only loaned her car to the guys who pulled the robbery. The cops that busted her found the loot and some dope in her closet during a search warrant. After that, I stopped caring and even forgot about her. She got some time for the caper."

"Evie had a daughter, about ten years old, she had out of wedlock. Later I found out she had an older girl too, who she had told me was her niece! What a fool she made of my ass!"

"Hey, we all get screwed up sometimes," Mel commented in an attempt to cheer up his gloomy partner.

"That ain't the whole story. When I just started working warrants, I stopped in at Highland Park station to check the Field Interrogation Card files on a person I was looking for. While I was in the files, I looked up Evie's name. There was nothing. I knew that couldn't be right, so I checked further and found a file on Sherry Barone, her daughter. It looked like the kid was going to follow in her mother's footsteps. Dope arrests, probation violations, heroin addiction."

"Then on the bottom of an FI card, I saw 'mother deceased.' It really blew my mind! I phoned the coroner's office and found out how Evie had died. She had been murdered by her doper common-law husband one month after having his baby! The report said that after an argument, the man had shot her in the head. Then he went out on the street and bragged to some of his friends that he had 'just shot his old lady.' He was convicted of voluntary manslaughter and got four years. Four fucking years for murder!" The two sat quiet for a couple of minutes.

"Are you okay?" asked Mel.

"Huh? Oh, yeah." he answered. "I'm fine. I was just thinking about the girl on this warrant."

"Gee, what a sad story. What are you going to do with the warrant?" he asked.

"I don't know. Let me think about it," answered the sullen cop.

The next day, Pete pulled the package on Sherry from the files upstairs in R&I. There were mug shots and other recent information. As Pete looked at the mug photos, he was amazed at how the young girl had changed. One shot showed her with dyed black hair. She obviously was trying to look like the Latino dopers she hung around with. Pete discovered that she actually had two wants out for her. One for violation of probation for dope and the other for hit-and-run!

He pulled the second warrant abstract from the files and added it to his folder. There was a recent business address listed in her folder. It was a clothing manufacturer in the downtown LA garment district. He went back downstairs with the information and met his partner.

"Here's the plan," Pete explained to Mel. "We go to her work address and talk to her, and if it's okay with you, we give her a month to take care of the warrants. If she doesn't, we bust her. How does that sound?" Mel agreed and they headed for the garment district.

The garment district of Los Angeles covers about a square mile of area between Wall Street on the east, Washington Boulevard on the south, Figueroa on the west, and Fifth Street on the north. It's not a pretty part of town, near what was called Skid Row. Mostly aliens work there. Uncle Ed used to shop there a lot because of the discounts on clothing he could get as a cop.

They pulled up in front of the small building on Fourteenth Street listed on the warrant. Inside, they talked to the boss who seemed like a nice sort. Pete told him the problem but minimized the seriousness of it. The cops asked if they could interview Sherry in private. The boss agreed and provided his office for the interview. When Sherry came in the door, she didn't have a clue what it was all about. When she saw the two men, she instantly recognized them as cops.

"Sherry," said Pete, "you don't remember me, do you? Pete Felix. I used to date your mother." Her eyes lit up with recognition.

"Sure," she said, "I do now. You're the motorcycle cop. It's been a long time."

"Yes it has. I know about your mother. What a shame. We had some good times together. Why don't you sit down? We need to talk." The potentially good-looking girl sat down, and Pete could tell the wheels were spinning in her head.

"Look, I just got this job a couple of months ago, and if I lose it, I'm screwed," she explained in a pleading voice. Pete had heard this line before, many times.

"You have two warrants out for your arrest. One for violation of probation and one for a hit-and-run."

"I know. I was supposed to go to court, but I didn't have any money to pay the fine and I didn't want to go to jail," she whined. The dark circles under her eye got darker as she started to sob.

"This is your lucky day, kid," said Pete. "In respect for your mother's memory, we're gonna give you a chance. You've got thirty days from today to take care of these warrants. Here's my card. If you take care of them sooner, call me. If I don't hear from you in thirty days, we'll have to come looking for you again. Fair enough?" Her eyes lit up again as she realized she wasn't going to jail.

"Thanks a lot. I really appreciate this. I'll take care of the warrants. I will, honest," she said with a childlike look that reminded him of someone he used to know.

"What do you hear from your old girlfriend's kid?" asked Mel about a month later.

"Shit," said Pete, "I had forgotten about her." He ran a check on the warrants in the computer.

"Still active," he advised. "Damn it. You can always tell when a doper is lying. Their lips move!" Pete got on the phone and called the place where Sherry worked. When she came to the phone, she was bubbling over with new excuses why she had not handled the warrants. Pete knew it was all bullshit. But he relented again.

"One more week," he said emphatically. "That's all!" He hung up.

A few days later, the phone rang in his office early in the morning.

"It's for you, Petey," said Billy. Pete picked up the phone. It was Sherry. New trouble.

"I couldn't help it," she cried. "The police car was coming down the street too fast!" she sobbed.

"You hit a police car?" asked Pete in a shocked voice. "Where? When?"

"Last night about seven thirty. I was pulling out of the liquor store parking lot. They hit me!" she said defensively.

"What's the deal then?" he asked, still not believing his ears.

"I walked out of the hospital," she said.

"You what? Another hit-and-run?"

"Well, I wasn't hurt, and anyway, those cops were speeding! Can you help me get my car out of the impound?" By this time, Pete's head was spinning. He needed to find out more before he said anything else.

"Look, I'll call you back later today. Where are you?"

"I'm living with my grandfather." She gave him the number. *Now she's bleeding the old man just like her mother did*, he thought. He got on the phone and called the Accident Investigation Unit that handles hit and run cases. He knew the officer that answered the phone. From him, he learned that Sherry had, in fact, been involved in a T/A with a patrol unit on its way to a call. They had sent her to the hospital for examination and treatment, and she had split from the hospital! The officers had not been hurt in the accident, but they were really pissed off!

The next day, Pete went up to the Highland Park station and talked to the officers who had been struck. He explained the situation and asked them if they would call off the hunt if he would get her to come into the hit-and-run unit. They hesitated and then agreed. Pete knew his ass was on the line now!

All this for her mother, and come to think of it, she had put his job in jeopardy by her conduct then went to jail! *Why am I doing all this shit?* He went back to the station and called the number Sherry had given him. When she answered, he told her the plan.

"I've made arrangements for you to meet with the accident investigation follow-up officers downtown. They want to question you and get your statement. If you do, they will call off the search for you." There was a long silence on the other end of the phone.

"I don't know," she said, hesitating.

"Well, you can do what you want. I'm just trying to help. You called me, remember?"

"Are you sure they won't arrest me?" she whined.

"I promise they won't," said Pete.

"Well, okay."

"Okay. Here's where to go and who to ask for," he said and he gave her the information. After she hung up, he called his friend in the follow-up unit.

"The hit-and-run suspect is coming in to talk to you about the accident. When she gets there, bust her and serve the other two warrants on her too," he said. *That was that*, he thought.

He felt like a creep for setting her up, but she would never do the right thing. Pete knew that. As long as she was out and getting high, she would never do the right thing.

Later, he was washing up in the locker room in the basement of the police building. He was alone and it was quiet. As he dried his hands with a paper towel, he looked at himself in the mirror. Sometimes he didn't like being a cop.

"I guess we have to be assholes, sometimes," he mumbled to himself.

Chapter Eight

"Bitch!" yelled Ronald. "I'll whup yo' ass!" The small black woman cringed in the corner, trying to ward off the blows from her drunken and drug-ridden boyfriend. It wasn't the first time Ronald had beaten her, and it wouldn't be the last. She knew it. But like many women, she took it. *Why?* she wondered. *I don't love him. I hate him! The motherfucker don't work. He don't do nothin' but give me grief,* she thought as she pleaded for mercy.

Finally, Ronald slapped her one last time across the face and left to go down to the corner to be with his friends. As Loretta tended to her wounds, she continued to think about her seven years of bad luck since coming to Los Angeles. She had suffered seven years of abuse—much of it violent abuse—from Ronald Stevens. He took her money and even her auntie's money and spent it on drugs and alcohol. Sure, he'd been in jail. But not for long. He always got out. *How did he do that?* she wondered. *Why didn't they lock him up and throw away the key? Someday I'll get even,* she swore. *Someday! But now, I gotta take care of Auntie, and we don't have no home except here at Ronald's place, so what can I do?*

In the meantime, Ronald roamed the streets. He'd been in jail many times, and like most career criminals, it held no terror for him. After all, that's where he met a lot of his friends, and that's where they made plans of what to do when they got out.

Ronald loved three things: alcohol, illegal drugs, and high-fashion clothes, all of which cost big bucks. So he kept active burglarizing of people's homes in the south central part of Los Angeles, stealing anything valuable and selling it to one of the shady "fences" who operated in the area. This got him his cash to buy dope and alcohol and more new clothes. He'd been busted for burglary, dope, and grand theft but had never served more than sixty days in the county jail for any of his criminal activities. Right now, there were several warrants out for Ronald's arrest in his own name and other fictitious names he'd used in Los Angeles and several different cities of the greater LA area. He couldn't remember how many.

He was a black man, thin and rather short in physical stature, with skinny birdlike legs. Ronald dressed well. He always had. His reputation for fashion went back to his high school days, where he had earned the nickname of "Slick." In spite of his diminutive size, he acted tough, especially around women. Ronald's took out his frustrations about his size and physique on his women. His "main squeeze" was Loretta Johnson, whom he brutalized frequently. She was a poor farmer's daughter who had come to California from Mississippi with her auntie several years ago.

Ronald was a local boy with the street smarts he had acquired growing up on the mean LA streets. Loretta was, in a way, over her head with Ronald, but she had nowhere to turn. She couldn't go back to Mississippi. The police? They were the enemy, at least that's what most of her people thought. That's what she'd always heard. She didn't know much about the law and warrants, but she was learning.

"Of all the assholes we look for, whores are the hardest to catch," complained Pete as he and Mel headed up the Pasadena Freeway toward the Highland Park Division. In his experience playing the hide-and-seek game, Pete had learned fast. Whores are hard to catch because they always give phony names and they move around every few weeks. Most of them live in hotels or motels and never leave forwarding addresses. The whore on this warrant had a real address!

"I can't believe we have a warrant for prostitution with an address in Highland Park," said Mel.

"Times, they are a changin'," quoted Pete.

Mel negotiated the twisting road that led up to the address in the hills above the Pasadena Freeway known as Montecito Hills.

"I hope we get to this address soon. I'm starting to get sick," whined Mel.

"Melvin the Seasick Sea Serpent," teased Pete.

"That's Cecil the Seasick Sea Serpent, and this ain't *Time for Beany* either. I hate twisty roads," whined Mel again.

"It's almost the same thing. A cop that gets carsick driving a police car!" Pete chuckled but felt a little sorry for Mel anyway.

The houses were all built on the sides of the hills here. Pete wondered why earthquakes hadn't knocked them all down. These were upper middle-class homes with a population of mixed ethnic groups but mostly Latinos. Mel pulled up in front of a neat-looking two-story house on a narrow winding street.

It was hot! Temperature near one hundred degrees today. In Los Angeles, temperatures that high are unusual, and Pete thanked God for the air-conditioning now provided in LAPD cars. Officers of the LAPD were convinced the city was always about five years behind other police departments in providing comfort for their officers. While most police departments were allowing their officers to wear short-sleeved shirts on their uniform, the LAPD held out until Chief Parker died in 1966. The officers had to wait a while longer for air-conditioning in the police cars.

Pete briefed Mel as they walked toward the house.

"We're looking for a female Negro, twenty-nine years old, black and brown, five foot four." Mel rang the doorbell as Pete made a routine check on the rear of the dwelling. There was no rear! The front of the house was at street level but because of the steep hillside, the back of the building was supported by *stilts*. This left the front door as the only way out, except for a side door Pete could see from the corner of the house. A walkway from the side door led to the front of the house.

Mel rang again. Pete looked up to the second-story windows and saw a black female face look down at them through the parted curtains. A look of recognition came over the face as she identified cops at her door. The curtain quickly closed. After ringing the doorbell and pounding on the door for several minutes, it was obvious that the woman was not coming out.

"Well, we can't go in on the probable cause we have right now," said Melvin disgusted.

"I'll hang a notice on the door, and we'll try to come back later and bag this bitch," said Pete.

They were both feeling the frustration that all officers feel when they know their suspect is in the house but they don't have enough "probable cause" to kick down the door. Pictures of the suspect sitting in the house, laughing at them flashed through their minds. As the cops walked back to their car, Pete had an idea.

"Did you notice that the circuit breaker box for that house was on the front?" asked Pete.

"No, I didn't."

"Let's go back and switch off the power in the house and the air-conditioning will shut off in there. Then we'll drive around the block and stake out on the ho."

"Let's do it!" said Mel with a twinkle in his eye. They walked back to the house and lifted the door on the circuit breaker box. Pete switched off the master breaker, and they heard the air-conditioning inside the house shut down. The two smiling cops walked back to their car and drove off. As soon as they were out of sight of the house, they quickly drove around the block and took up a position where they could see the house but could not be seen readily. They waited. Five minutes. Ten. After about fifteen minutes, the front door of the house opened and a sweat-covered black face peeked out to see if the officers had gone. Seeing no cops, the woman went to the circuit breaker box to see why the power had gone off. While she was trying to figure it out, Mel and Pete slipped up and pounced on her. She didn't put up a fight but only protested the "illegal" and "unfair' way they had suckered her out of the house. The two partners had a good laugh over it, and the frustration melted away.

Chapter Nine

Pete was notified that the trial of the man who had tried to run him off the Pomona Freeway was set for next week. He told his sergeant that he had to be in court on an off-duty caper. The department doesn't like off-duty capers so the sergeant wasn't too happy.

He took the trip out to Pomona, where the case was to be tried. The deputy district attorney prosecuting the case turned out to be an old friend of his. As he walked into the DDA's office, Henry Harpster stood up to greet him with a handshake.

"Just can't stay out of trouble, huh?" said the tall, slightly balding man in his early forties. "Sit down and have a cup of coffee." Pete sat down in a chair and tried to relax. He didn't like being in the position he was in. It was awkward.

The deputy DA continued, "Well, sometimes trouble comes to you and doesn't give you much choice in the matter. In my opinion, you should have shot the son of a bitch. Fewer reports and less cost for the county."

"Easy to say now. I thought about it at the time, but with my luck, I'd have missed and nailed some old lady driving home from church. Then her car would have gone out of control and killed a black family."

The DDA chuckled and nodded his head. "We've got a strong case against this creep, and I'm going to handle it myself, unless you have a problem with that?"

"Hell no, Henry. But I don't want to put you in a compromising position."

"Not a problem. We'll hang this asshole together." Pete had learned when anyone says "not a problem," that's the time to start worrying.

The day of the trial came. Pete sat in court looking at the now clean-shaven face of the man who had tried to kill him. His name was William Collins, and he looked just like anyone else in the courtroom. Suit and tie. Very respectable. He had even brought his wife and children to court with him! Pete suspected that was a suggestion from his defense attorney to sway the jury.

Pete had been around long enough to know the defense's strategy: show the jury a completely different person than the prosecution's testimony would describe. The jury would see and might even sympathize with this kindly husband and father accused of being an uncaring beast that would run over a man on a motorcycle and leave him to be hit by a few hundred other cars on the busy freeway. Hearing that accusation presented, even with evidence to support it, they would ask themselves, "How could such a nice-looking, well-dressed man do such a thing?" People on juries look at the person's appearance and make judgments. The defense will capitalize on that fact, if it can, in criminal cases.

Pete had known that when the DDA said "no problem," there would have to be a problem, and here it was sitting on "the bench." The judge picked to try the case was definitely going to be the problem. She had never handled a felony trial in her life! In addition, according to Henry Harpster, she wasn't even qualified to be a judge. The governor had appointed her because she was (1) female and (2) a female liberal Democrat. Those were her main qualifications. She had handled nothing but civil cases prior to Pete's case. *Judge Rose wasn't even good-looking*, thought Pete! The warning bells started going off in his head about the trial.

After the jury was selected, the trial settled down into the routine. Direct testimony and cross-examination of Pete. He testified to the facts of the case and how it had progressed from a minor traffic confrontation to a felony. He had to be very careful not to overplay the fact that he was a police officer. He played the role of the "poor guy riding his motorcycle who was attacked for no apparent reason by this maniac." This was easy to do because that's what had actually happened!

Pete had always been a good witness in court. Years of experience had taught him how to present facts in a case and how to look at the jury when he answered questions. To think before he answered. To hesitate when the defense asked an objectionable question so the prosecution could object. He also was wise to a typical defense attorney's trick questions and knew how to avoid giving them the answers they wanted. It was sort of a game. But with an inexperienced judge like this one, he had to be very careful.

"Now Officer Felix," said the defense attorney with emphasis on the word *officer*, "when you turned and looked at the defendant driving the car you say swerved at you. You testified you gave him a thumbs-up sign with your left thumb. Is that correct?"

"Yes, it is."

"Isn't it a fact that you made an obscene gesture, commonly known as 'the finger'?"

"No. That is not correct. I was on a motorcycle and completely exposed. I do not give people reasons to hurt me by provoking them."

"It made you mad when Mr. Collins, according to you, swerved at you didn't it?"

"It was cause for alarm and made me take evasive actions to protect myself."

"Isn't it a fact that you tried to run Mr. Collins off the road?"

"Sir, do you really think a seven-hundred-pound motorcycle has the capability to force a two or three-thousand-pound automobile off the road, sir?"

"Please answer the question with a yes or no Officer Felix," the judge sneered.

"The answer is no."

"You testified that you threatened Mr. Collins with a gun. Is that correct Officer Felix?"

"No. I testified that I used my police weapon to defend myself."

"Are you carrying that weapon today?"

"Yes, I am."

"Your Honor, I would like to have Officer Felix's pistol admitted in evidence," stated the defense attorney.

"Officer Felix, will you please turn your gun over to the bailiff," said the judge.

Pete could hardly believe his ears! He darted a quick look at Harpster, who appeared to be in shock. Then he came to life!

"Your Honor," said the DDA, jumping up from his seat, "this is absurd! Officer Felix is not on trial here! His police weapon is part of his required equipment. He's required to carry it."

The judge looked bewildered for a second, as though she had forgotten who was on trial. Then she realized she had made an error.

"Your request is denied, Counsel." She sat back in her seat and hunched down as if to hide for a few minutes while the trial went on. There were several other objections and motions made during the trial. The judge actually had to leave the bench on two occasions to "go and check the law" in her chambers.

"God help us," whined Pete as the court was reconvened after a recess.

"Don't worry," said Harpster. "We're doin' fine. This jury is eating up your story."

The defendant took the stand. He lied like no one has ever lied before. According to him, Pete had nearly hit his car on the freeway. Then when he honked at the motorcycle the rider made obscene gestures and yelled obscenities at him and his passenger. They tried to get away from Pete, but he followed and tried to run them off the road with his motorcycle and threatened them with a gun. They were afraid to stop so they tried to get away, and Pete shot out the tire.

The whole story was just the reverse of the truth, and it was the defendant's word against his. But that story was too much for even a jury to buy. After a short deliberation, they brought in a verdict of guilty. The defendant was ordered to return for sentencing in two weeks.

"Thanks for your help in convicting this asshole," said Pete as he and the DDA walked out of the courthouse. "For a while I was worried. Juries are unpredictable."

"Your solid testimony and the fact that no one could buy the idea of a motorcycle running a car off the road was enough to hang his ass. He should get some time. What do you think is fair?"

"Well," Pete thought for a moment, "The guy has no record to speak of. But I think he should at least get thirty days. That way his felony conviction will become a misdemeanor, and maybe he'll learn a lesson."

"Sounds fair to me. I'll push for it at the sentencing. See ya around, Pete."

Pete went back to work and didn't think much of the trial until he got a call from District Attorney Harpster. Cops learn never to attend the sentencing of people they arrest because it would look like they had too much of a personal interest in the case, or so they are told. Cops are not supposed to care if the bad guy gets off or not.

"Well, Pete," said the DDA, "He got three years' summary probation."

"You're shittin' me! Probation with no requirements to report to a probation officer! No jail time at all? I can't believe it!" Pete's head started to throb, and his blood pressure must have gone to about two hundred.

"Thanks to our Honorable Judge Rose, that's it," replied Harpster.

Pete was speechless for several seconds. "Well, at least the asshole will think of me every day."

"What do you mean, Pete?"

"Every morning when the son of a bitch combs his hair and the comb bounces over those bumpy scars I put there, he'll remember me."

"Stay out of trouble, Pete."

"Thanks, Henry."

The policy of the LAPD prohibited officers from shooting at moving vehicles unless it was necessary to save the officer's or someone else's life. Pete's use of his weapon to stop the vehicle driven by the driver who was attempting to run Pete off of the road went before a "use of force" review board. The board ruled that Pete's actions were justified under the circumstance. That was a relief to Pete, who could not predict how the department would rule on his actions.

Chapter Ten

Pete and Mel pulled away from the gas pumps at PAB and drove east on First Street toward the Hollenbeck Division.

"Let's go out into the county today, Melvin. I've got a couple of warrants we need to recheck, okay?"

Mel was opening up the brown paper sack on the seat next to him as he drove. He pulled out a slice of a carrot with his right hand while steering the car with his left. He popped the carrot into his mouth and, with a loud crunch, took a large bite of it. Mel knew Pete would be staring at him because that's what always happened when Mel was eating something Pete didn't like. Mel savored the taste of the vegetable audibly with a long drawn-out "Mmmmmm," trying to needle Pete.

"You're going to turn yellow if you keep eating that fucking rabbit food."

"Have one," offered Mel.

"I'd rather eat a dog turd. Later, we'll go to Al and Bea's burrito stand and have some real food. Some *burritos con frijoles, caso y chile verde, hombre!*"

"I do like those burritos," said Mel, admitting grudgingly. "You've already spoiled part of my routine since you made me eat those burritos."

"I *made* you eat 'em? You jumped on 'em like a duck on a June bug, buddy!"

"Yeah. I never thought I'd like Mexican food."

"At least those carrots haven't destroyed your total mental capacity. Let's go see if our contractor is home today."

The "contractor" was a suspect on a warrant for construction contracting without a license. The bail was $10,000! Pete had thought the bail was excessive until he took the time to look into the case more closely. The contractor was one of those crooks you hear about once in a while on the news. He does construction jobs for people who haven't taken the trouble to learn that he doesn't have a contractor's license. He covers up his inferior materials and poor workmanship with cheap paint and collects the money. Pretty soon, the poor victim finds out he's been ripped off when the whole thing falls apart. By that time, the "contractor" has disappeared. This guy was one of those and Pete and Mel wanted him badly.

They had gone to his home several times before, only to be told he was not at home. The suspect's police package told the cops that this bogus contractor owned a white Ford pickup and the cops had its license number. On all the occasions they had been to the house, the suspect's son had told them his father wasn't home. On those occasions, they had not seen the white truck near the house, but today there it was! The white Ford pickup. Pete's heart started to beat faster.

"Melvin, I'll go to the front door while you watch the back, okay?" Mel nodded. They parked down the block about a hundred feet from the house and walked up slowly and watchfully.

"I want this asshole," said Pete to himself.

As they came to the front door, Pete hesitated until Mel was in place then knocked loudly on the front door. As before, the same boy opened the door as the times before. He appeared to be about fifteen.

"Hi," said Pete. "Remember me? Go tell your dad I want to talk to him. I know he's here because his truck is outside, so just go upstairs and tell him to come down." Pete didn't really know if the guy was upstairs or not but the kid didn't know that. The kid hesitated for a few seconds, thinking of what to do. That told Pete that the suspect was probably upstairs.

"If you don't go get him, I'll have to do it."

The kid stood frozen to the spot, not knowing what to do. A loud noise came from upstairs. The kid had a look of panic on his face. Quickly, he slammed the door and locked it! That was P/C enough for Pete! He yelled at Mel that he was going in and backed up to kick the door. The problem was the door was up a step from ground level where Pete stood so he would have to kick several inches higher than he normally would to hit the spot near the doorknob. It put him off balance.

His kick missed and went to the left, hitting the thin wood panel next to the knob. Crunch! The panel gave way, and Pete's foot went through the door half way to his knee! Mel was somewhere to the rear of the house and that left Pete by himself, dangling from the door, with right leg sunk into it about twelve inches!

Pete couldn't get his leg out! He jerked and tugged, but the leg was stuck! Since he had kicked high, he was now stuck there doing the splits and very much off balance! Pete's mind visualized his leg breaking if he fell backward. Then another thought flashed through his mind. A thought that made him shiver. A vision of someone on the other side of the door, someone very mad at cops, chopping off the leg sticking through his door with a large machete! That did it!

In desperation, Pete threw his weight backward with all his might. *Better a broken leg than no leg at all*, he thought! He went crashing to the ground as the leg came loose from the door panel. He felt a searing pain in his leg as the jagged edges of the door stripped skin from his shin. He staggered to his feet, and finding his leg bleeding but still operable, limped over to where he had last seen his partner running. In the distance, he saw Mel walking back toward him with a handcuffed man in tow. Pete breathed a sigh of relief.

Mel had seen the suspect climbing out of an upstairs back window and had chased the wanted man down after running about a block. Mel, who ran marathons, wasn't even breathing hard. As he walked up with his prisoner, he smiled.

"And if you eat your carrots, you can catch suspects too," he said in the high-pitched voice he used to piss Pete off. This time Pete just laughed and then winced as he looked at his scratched and bleeding shinbone.

Pete wondered what had happened to Sherry Barone since he had set her up for arrest on the two warrants and the hit-and-run charge. He'd felt badly about it but knew it had to be done. Otherwise, she'd never get straightened out. She had been on the methadone program, which, to Pete, was just a way for government to provide synthetic dope to addicts. He really doubted that anyone had ever been saved from heroin by the methadone program.

He checked to find out the disposition of her case. He found out she was serving a ninety-day sentence in Sybil Brand Institute for Women (SBI), located in the hills of East Los Angeles.

Walking up to the gate at SBI, he wondered what the hell he was doing here. This chick really meant nothing to him. Maybe he was feeling guilty about setting her up or maybe he hoped he could help her in some way. He didn't know. He checked his pistol at the entrance and went in. Being an officer, he didn't have to go through the same routine others did in order to visit a prisoner. As far as the Sheriff's Department knew, he was interviewing a witness.

After a twenty-minute wait, Sherry came into the interview room. She had changed. Her hair was darker in color and she had put on weight and she looked healthier than the last time Pete had seen her. She looked . . . good. She frowned when she saw him, and Pete thought he was probably in for trouble.

"Hello, Sherry. How're you doin'?" She couldn't really refuse to see him since he was a cop and here to interview her.

"I'm okay. What have I done now?"

"Nothing. I just wanted to see how you were doing. And if there's anything I can do for you," he said. She relaxed a little.

"Look, I know you're mad at me for settin' you up," Pete confessed, "but where was this going? When was it going to end? You had no intention of turning yourself in, did you?" She sat down in a chair.

"I thought you were trying to help me," she said.

"I *am* trying to help you. But I can't do it if you keep getting into trouble with the law. I had warrants on you. Don't you understand that I couldn't ignore them forever? I was breaking the law myself just by sitting on them for as long as I did!" He watched for a break in her sour expression. "I can only do so much, and then it's up to you. And you weren't doing anything."

"Well, maybe you're right. I knew I'd get busted sooner or later. It's my own fault, I guess."

Pete saw the change in her face. "Look, you're a nice-looking young woman. You're young and can still turn your life around and make something of yourself. If you want to, that is."

"Well, at least when I get out I won't have those warrants worrying me. I'm kicking my habit in here. I've been clean now for a month," she said proudly.

"Great! Now keep it up, and when you get out, I'll see what I can do to help you get your job back. Is there anything I can do for you while you're here?"

"Well, I don't have any money. A couple of bucks would be nice." Pete took a five-dollar bill out of his pocket and handed it to the young woman.

"Thanks," she said. "Got any gum?" Pete just happened to have a pack and gave it to her.

"Are you coming to see me again?" she asked.

"Sure, if you'd like me to, I will."

"Yeah, I'd like that."

"Okay. Maybe next week. Take care and hang in, okay?"

"Bye," she said. As she walked away, Pete thought about her mother, Evie. He walked out of SBI and inhaled the fresh air of the outside. *Jail must be hell,* he thought. Why was he doing this? He wouldn't tell any of the guys at work about his visit. *They'd just accuse him of trying to get in her pants,* he thought. He really wasn't interested in that. He decided he was probably a little soft-hearted about the kid. What a life she'd had! Not much of a chance. *Everyone deserved a chance,* he thought.

Chapter Eleven

"Any unit in the vicinity, shots fired from the hotel at Seventh and Columbia Street," squawked the police radio in Pete and Mel's car. They were going south on Alvarado Street, approaching Sixth Street.

"Wanna roll on that?" asked Pete. Mel accelerated and made a left on Seventh. As the two plainclothes cops came in from the west, a Rampart black-and-white was stopping at the corner about a half block from the hotel. The hotel was one of those semi-run-down brick places that had survived since the early twenties. Six or seven stories high, it was now the habitat of low-income working Latinos and old pensioners who couldn't afford to live anywhere else.

"Shop 285 is code 6 at Seventh and Columbia in plain clothes," said Pete into the microphone. Mel pulled up behind the black-and-white patrol car.

"Hi, guys," said Pete as they got out to back up the two patrol cops. A man came toward them from the hotel. He was staying close to the building and glancing up now and then.

"There's a guy up there shooting at people on the street. He's up on the fourth floor of this hotel," said the excited man.

"Which room is he in?" asked one of the uniformed cops.

The man pointed upward. "He shot from the fourth floor, the window on that corner," said the man, again pointing upward. The window was open, but the men could see no one there. The four cops moved toward the hotel door, keeping close to the wall of the building. Apparently the sniper had hit no one, yet.

As the cops moved into the lobby of the hotel, they formulated their strategy. It was pretty simple. They had to go up and get the sniper before he fired any more shots. The quicker the shooter was taken out, the safer it would be. Pete didn't want this to turn into a hostage or barricaded suspect situation. *Once SWAT was called in, the whole thing would go to shit*, thought Pete. One officer was left in the lobby to keep it clear and to make sure no one got out.

"Let's go," said Pete as he led Mel and the other cop to the stairway. *What the hell am I doing up in front?* he asked himself as they started up the dark stairway to the fourth floor. Pete and Mel and the uniformed cop drew their guns and held them at the ready.

The stairway was steep and narrow, and the stairs creaked loudly as the cops ascended slowly. Pete's mind flashed pictures of movie scenes where cops get shot in stairways like this. There was a door at the top of each flight of stairs. The first three floors had been empty when the cops carefully opened the doors. They were now approaching the fourth-floor door. Pete looked up at the door. His hand hefted the heavy pistol it held. His heart was pumping like crazy and not just from climbing the stairs. What if the sniper was waiting for them to open the door? Pete was the first one in line. He wished he'd worn his bulletproof vest. Too late now.

As Pete reached up to open the door, it was pulled open from the other side. A dark figure with a long object in his hand stood silhouetted in the doorway. Pete jumped back and leveled his pistol at the man, starting to put pressure on the trigger. Once again his experience told him to wait a second. The "rifle" the person carried was pointed at the floor. Pete yelled, "Drop it!"

The wooden cane fell to the floor, and the old black man raised his hands as he stared into the muzzles of three pistols. Pete breathed a sigh of relief and lowered his gun.

"Wha's de trouble, Office?" asked the old man. Pete moved into the hall followed by the other two.

"We have a report of a man shooting from a window of this floor. Where do you stay, Pops?" The three cops were still looking up and down the hall in case the sniper came out.

"I stays in room 427, right over dere," said the old man, pointing to the corner room. The cops looked at each other. They accompanied the old man back to his room and discovered that his room was the window on the corner! They searched and found a .22 rifle in the closet. It had been recently fired. The old man went to jail.

"What if the old fart had been carrying the rifle when he opened that door?" asked Mel later as they left the police building after filling out reports on the old sniper.

"Shit, I almost shot him anyway for carrying a cane! I was really glad it turned out to be a cane, and then it turns out he's the asshole shooting out the window! Life gets complicated, don't it?"

Pete was out on his own today and picked some warrant abstracts in the Hollywood area. Back when he was a motor cop, Pete enjoyed this area but noticed that it was rapidly deteriorating into a drug and prostitute-infested part of the city that still had a romantic name.

Pete had to chuckle to himself as he recalled the time when he was patrolling "The Boulevard" as Hollywood Boulevard was called by the cops who worked there. Pete had noticed that most people will believe mostly anything a police officer tells them. He playfully decided to try an experiment one day.

As he rode along on his police motorcycle, he saw a young man walking on the sidewalk close to the curb. Pete pulled up and stopped his motorcycle. He beeped his horn to attract the man's attention and said, "Pull over to the wall."

The man stopped and moved over to the wall of the building there.

"What's the trouble, Officer," the man asked with a look of disbelief.

Pete got off of his motorcycle and casually pulled his gloves off one finger at a time with a serious look on his face.

"You were taking ten steps in a five-step zone, sir!"

"You mean there's a speed limit for walking now?" asked the man with his arms outstretched.

"Yes! It's a new law passed because people were walking too fast and bumping into other people and several accidents have occurred as a result," advised Pete as he looked the man in the eye.

"You see those separation lines in the sidewalk?" Pete continued. "You are only allowed five steps between those lines," as he pointed to the expansion lines in the cement walk.

"Gosh, Officer! I didn't know! I'm new in town."

"Well, because you're new and it's a new law, I'm just giving you a warning today. But try to be more careful in the future."

"Oh, thank you, Officer! I really appreciate that!"

Pete put his gloves back on in the same deliberate manner in which he had taken them off and remounted his police motorcycle. As he rode away, Pete could hardly keep from falling off of his motor from laughing! His suspicions were confirmed.

The warrant was issued for a man with the last name of Gupta, a rather common Indian name. As Pete rolled up to the address on the warrant, he noticed that this particular neighborhood was once a ritzy part of Hollywood. This street was located a couple of blocks north of Hollywood Boulevard and ran parallel to it. The house was big and old, and Pete guessed it was built in the early 1920s or earlier perhaps. It looked in good shape but was painted a weird color of light purple!

Pete approached the door and knocked. A maid answered the door, and Pete identified himself. The maid went into the interior of the home, and voices were heard. A dark-skinned man of short stature greeted the officer.

"Come in. What can I do for you, Officer?" asked the man with very little foreign accent. From the inside furnishings of the house, it was obvious to Pete that this man was well healed.

"Are you Depak Gupta, sir?"

"Yes!" answered the man, now appearing to get anxious.

"I have a warrant for your arrest for health and safety code violations in your apartment building."

"What do you mean a warrant for me?"

"It means a judge in a court of law says to arrest you and bring you to jail. Your bail is set at $500.00."

The man looked upset and started to pace the floor. "I don't know what this is all about, but I pay you now and you go away, yes?"

Pete patiently explained that bail was only accepted at the jail in downtown Los Angeles. The arrest went smoothly and Mr. Gupta went quietly, although he continued to complain all the way down to the Central Jail. Pete did not handcuff the man.

On the way, Pete tried to distract the man from his anger by opening a conversation.

"Your house is really a classic Hollywood home. When was it built?" he asked.

"My house used to belong to Al Jolson many years ago. It was built in 1920 something, I think," answered Mr. Gupta.

"Wow! You mean the famous singer?" exclaimed Pete, purposely overacting to keep his prisoner off guard. Pete was not in the mood to have a suspect in his custody that might become violent with him. Contrary to what most people think, even one man who is resisting an officer can be dangerous, and Pete wanted no part of any confrontation with Mr. Gupta, who appeared to be rather wealthy and capable of slapping a lawsuit on him. So Pete continued to be friendly and engaging all the way to the Central Jail at Parker Center on Los Angeles Street.

During the booking, Gupta continued to complain about why he had to be "booked" before he could pay his bail. He waived a large roll of bills around until the jailer made him place them on the counter. Gupta was booked and Pete left the jail after telling his arrestee that he could not drive him back to his Hollywood house. Once the arrestee has posted bail, Pete could not transport him home. It was forbidden to carry passengers who are not in custody or authorized to ride in police vehicles. *Besides*, Pete mused to himself, *Gupta probably had enough money on him to buy a car to drive himself home!*

While watching an evening news broadcast on TV at home later that week, an arrest of a big "slum lord" was being covered. He owned a large, old run-down apartment house at Vermont Avenue, near the Hollywood Freeway underpass. Low and behold, a familiar face appeared on the TV screen.

"Hey, honey! Come look at this," he called to his wife in the kitchen. "I busted this guy about a week ago on a warrant for a health department violation. I've been in the cruddy apartment house he owns and it was really bad! Gee, it is nice to know this jerk is now in deeper shit than the little five-hundred-dollar warrant I busted him on." Pete thought that once in a while, he got to see some of the good things that he did in serving warrants.

"The Phantom strikes again!" said Pete's wife, kidding him a little. *It's nice to have a wife that appreciates police work*, he thought sarcastically as he stood up and flexed his biceps for her. She walked back into the kitchen, ignoring Pete, and returned to her work without further comment.

Chapter Twelve

"You're gonna build a what?" asked Pete's wife as she stopped what she was doing in the kitchen and turned around to face her husband. Pete and one of his ex-partners from motors had been talking about the project for some time, but this was the first time he had mentioned it to Noel.

"We're gonna build gyrocopters and fly 'em in the desert," he explained to his wife. "They're the latest thing in personal experimental aircraft. Bill Haymes and I are each going to build one."

"What the hell is it?" she repeated. Like many wives whose husbands come up with what sound like harebrained ideas, Noel took a negative attitude from the beginning.

Pete had been riding motorcycles in the desert for years. They had gone on many trips to the Mojave Desert to ride dirt bikes on the dry lakes there. To Noel, it was dirty, usually uncomfortable, and not her idea of the most pleasant of outings. In the morning, you froze and by noon you were roasting in the desert sun! The kids usually had fun shooting guns with their dad and taking short rides on small motorbikes, but generally Noel thought the whole thing was a pain. She had been happy that the desert riding days appeared to be over. Now Pete springs another project that sounds really dangerous.

"A gyrocopter is a little aircraft that looks like a helicopter but it's not," said Pete, trying to shape one with his hands in the air. "Auto gyros have been around since the twenties but have faded out over the years. Now someone has invented a small version of the auto gyro that can be built in your garage. You start out by building a glider and then later you put a motor in it and fly it." It all sounded simple and exciting to Pete. Noel had a different attitude.

"Don't forget . . . what goes up . . . must come down. That's the part I worry about. How it comes down. Can't you find something a little more . . . normal to do? Why not build furniture in the garage? Something practical and useful. Why are all your projects life-threatening? Isn't being a cop enough risk for you, you gotta build a flying thing?"

"You sound like a Jewish mother, vat da hell," chuckled Pete.

"That's because I worked in a Jewish bakery when I was a kid and I think like a Jewish mother. What does Bill's wife think about his crazy idea?"

"It's not a crazy idea, and she probably thinks the same way you do, but we've decided we're gonna do this. We saw some of them flying the last time we went to El Mirage Dry Lake, remember?"

"Those little things that look like a lawn chair with a whirly gig on top?" she asked in a high-pitched voice. "You gotta be kidding?" she said, her voice getting a little louder.

"Now calm down. They're safe to fly, and it is gonna be a lot of fun."

"For who? It won't be fun for me when you're lying in a bed in some rest home with the IQ of a rutabaga because you fell out of your flying lawn chair onto the dry lake!"

"You always have such a refreshing way of expressing yourself," said Pete, trying to maintain a straight face and be serious. "We're gonna do this safely and slowly so we don't end up as rutabagas, so relax." Noel could see it was useless to argue and threw up her hands and walked away in disgust at the whole idea.

So the project went into full swing. The two cops bought a set of plans and directions for the construction of the gyros and went to work in Bill's garage. Bill had a good set of power and hand tools and was very good at working with them. Pete was not as gifted but had a lot of enthusiasm for the project.

The primary frame for the aircraft consisted of two-inch square aluminum tubing held together with aircraft nuts and bolts. The rotor blades had to be handmade of laminated wood of several kinds and required careful and accurate shaping. It was going to be a long project, but the two cops looked forward to the adventure of flight.

Once a year, the Los Angeles Police Department held a big inspection to assure that field personnel had all the proper and required equipment to do their job. Each bureau and division commander was required to inspect the officers for proper uniforms, weapons, handcuffs, batons, and all the other tools a cop uses in the field. The formal inspection was generally for uniformed personnel. Because detectives and others work in plain clothes instead of a uniform, their inspection was informal and usually done by their immediate supervisor without having to stand in a formation in uniform.

"Well, men," said Sergeant Wilson, the Warrant Detail's supervisor, "I guess we'll have to stand this inspection in uniform."

"Whadda ya mean, Sarge?" asked Billy Much with a screwed up expression on his face. "We don't wear uniforms!"

"Yeah," said Pete, "the guys up in Fugitive and Bunco Forgery don't have to stand inspection in uniform. Why do we? We work in plain clothes too!"

"Because they're detectives and you guys are only P-2s, that's why," said the sergeant in a sarcastic manner. Sergeant Wilson was not really well liked by the men whom he supervised. He always seemed to be aloof from their problems and appeared to be coasting toward his retirement like several others in the detail. Pete had little respect for "coasters."

"So what you're saying is that the Warrant Detail that works the field in plain clothes just like the dicks will be treated differently only because we are of a lower rank?" stated Pete.

"Felix, why do you always take an order and twist it so it sounds bad?" asked Wilson.

"Because some of them are stupid orders and they're not fair, that's why."

"Well, whether you think it's fair or not, you will stand at your desk on inspection day in full uniform and equipment. That's the way it is," said the sergeant with a smirk.

The men in the unit objected to the order not just because they would have to wear uniforms but because most of the guys hadn't been in the field uniform for years and had let their uniforms deteriorate. In Pete's case, he said his uniform had "shrunk" while it had been hanging in his closet for the past two years since he had left motors. Pete and several other officers in the unit had to go out and buy practically a whole new uniform for the inspection. It was costly.

The day of the inspection came, and the men were standing around, waiting for the commander and his entourage to arrive. Pete looked around the room at the men in uniform. They all had a least three hash marks on their sleeves. D. J. Willis had four, indicating at least twenty years on the job. Pete was only a few months away from his twenty. He could hardly wait!

Getting your twenty in meant a lot to the cops. It meant your pension was vested, which is the major goal of most cops on LAPD. It also meant you joined the ranks of a few elite on the job that "can't be fired." Although that's not really true, it is nearly the same. Once an officer has passed his twentieth anniversary he, or she, can still be fired, but the pension can't be taken away. So, too many twenty-year cops develop an "I don't care" attitude about the job.

For Pete, it meant a lot, but he had vowed to himself that when he got his twenty in, it wouldn't make him indifferent to his duty. He hated cops who had an indifferent attitude to police work. *If they didn't want to arrest bad guys, then they should get the hell out of the field, or quit*, he thought!

"Here they come," warned the sergeant. "Everyone stand by your desks." Pete felt angry all of a sudden. *What the hell are we doing? This is dumb and childish*, he thought.

"I have to pee, Sarge," said Billy Much. The sergeant scowled at him.

"Hey, Sarge," whispered Pete loudly, "are they gonna inspect our fingernails to see if they are clean too?" The sergeant glared at him too.

"Oh, for Christ's sake," mumbled Pete under his breath.

The commander was a real man who was well liked by the street cops and had been around and came up through the ranks. He was obviously as uncomfortable with the situation as the men in uniform were. He cleared his throat as he looked around the room at the group of veteran officers standing by their tables.

"Boy, there are a lot of hash marks in this room," he stammered. Pete's anger was smoldering and his face was turning red. Just then the alarm on Pete's wristwatch went off with a beeping noise. Pete forgot he had set it for 7:00 a.m., the time he and Mel usually left the office for breakfast.

"Sorry, commander, your time is up," Pete blurted out as he looked at his watch and shut off the alarm. Pete then headed for the door. Mel followed.

The commander stood there frozen for a second, then as Pete passed by him on his way out, he said, "You must be Felix."

"Yes, sir! Have a nice day."

The captain was getting red in the face but kept his mouth shut. Pete and Mel went to the academy for breakfast. Billy Much and his partner caught up with them there later.

"Petey, you sure pissed off the supervisors that time! The only thing that saved your ass was the Commander thought it was funny. After you guys left, I heard him talking to the sergeant and the captain. He told them to forget it."

"Well, hell! It was embarrassing standing there like a bunch of rookies! That's bullshit," said Pete.

"You made them think though. Maybe next time, we'll have a different kind of inspection. Thanks, Petey!" said Billy in his usual obnoxious way.

"Don't call me Petey, asshole."

Pete pulled up to the curb in the parking lot of the housing project near East Ninth Street and Olympic Boulevard known as Wyvernwood. He had a warrant for a young male Latino named Guerrero for drunk driving. He was working alone today and had picked out warrants that looked mild in nature. He really didn't want any trouble.

As he walked up to the door of the address on the warrant, he noticed a potted plant sitting on the inside windowsill inside the window of the apartment where he was about to knock. It was a marijuana plant! *Man*, thought Pete, *these guys are either dumb or just don't give a shit!* He knocked on the door. The curtain parted slightly as someone peeked out to see who was at the door. Then a woman's hand appeared in the window and grabbed the plant off the sill.

"I'm Officer Felix, LAPD," advised Pete as he showed the young Latino woman his ID card. "Is Jorge Guerrero home?" The woman seemed cool and collected.

"No, he's at work," she answered in perfect English. "What's the matter?" she asked.

"I have a warrant for his arrest for drunk driving and failure to appear."

"Well, he said he's saving his money to pay for that ticket that's why he didn't come down."

Pete filled out a warrant notification form and gave it to the woman.

"By the way," said Pete, "where's the plant that was in the window?"

"What plant?" asked the woman in an innocent tone.

"Okay, I don't have time for games so listen up. There was a marijuana plant in the window when I knocked on your door. Someone in this apartment took the plant out of the window. You are the only one here, I presume, so you've got two choices. Either you bring me the plant right now or I will search the house until I find it. If I search, I just might come up with a lot more stuff you don't want me to find, so the choice is yours."

"But don't you need a warrant to search?" she asked.

"Not when I just saw illegal contraband in plain view, I don't."

"It's not mine," she said. "It's my brother's plant."

"I don't care whose it is. It's yours now! It's in your possession." The woman went to the closet and took out the plant and put it on the table. Pete's mind was calculating what to do now. If he busted the woman for cultivating the illegal plant it would mean court time, which would probably end up in probation for the woman. The plant was only about twelve inches high anyway. *To hell with it*, he thought!

"Here's the deal," said Pete, "you take that pair of scissors on the table over there and cut that plant into little pieces right now. You flush it down the toilet, and we'll forget about the whole thing."

"My brother will really be mad at me."

"Like, I give a shit? Well, then put your hands behind your back so I can put these handcuffs on you, and let's go to jail."

"Wait, wait," she begged. She grabbed the scissors and started to cut the plant into bits. Pete watched until the plant was totally destroyed.

As he walked back to his car he wondered how people could be so arrogant as to have a marijuana plant in the window in plain sight! It must not be an uncommon thing here or else someone would report it to the police. Then he thought again, *Not likely*. And he guessed it wouldn't get any better in the future.

Chapter Thirteen

Mel parked the car quietly at the curb about half a block away from the address on the warrant they were trying to serve. It was just another routine warrant stop for the two hide-and-seek players. Pete gave Mel the rundown on the suspect.

"This is a male Negro aged thirty-four, five feet six, wanted for violating probation for violation of probation for dope," read Pete in a dull voice.

It had also been a dull day so far, and Pete was looking forward to end of watch and the weekend. Pete approached the front door as Mel started around the side of the house to cover the back. But instead of going all the way to the back, Mel stopped about halfway alongside of the house. Pete thought Mel had time to reach the back door by now and knocked on the front door.

The door had one of those little peek holes with a small door that opened from the inside. The miniature door opened, and a female face filled the space.

"What choo wont?"

"Police, ma'am. I'd like to speak to Ronald Stevens, please."

"He ain't here right now." Pete saw her eyes moving to her left, as if she was trying to tell him to look there. A man got up from the couch and headed for the back of the house. He seemed in a hurry.

"Mel!" yelled Pete. "He's headed your way!" Pete backed up and kicked the front door. The latch gave way, and the door slammed open. The woman jumped out of the way as Pete ran through the house after the running suspect. Pete's mind raced. *We don't even know if this is the guy. It could be someone else who's wanted. But for what?*

He yelled again for Mel, who he thought was in rear of the house. But Mel wasn't in the back. He had heard Pete yell but hadn't understood what was happening so had come back around the front. As Pete grabbed for the fleeing suspect, the man jumped out an open back window then jumped over the back fence and was gone!

"Shit, Mel, where the hell were you?" growled Pete at his embarrassed partner. He hated to lose a suspect, and he was pissed at Mel. "Dammit, Partner! We had the son of a bitch!"

"I heard you yell, and I thought you were in trouble so I came back around to help."

Then Pete started to feel like a jerk. Mel had only been thinking of his partner.

"Aw, forget it, Mel. We'll get the asshole later." Pete was still pissed and was now really determined to get this dude.

About a week passed. One morning, as Mel and Pete were sorting warrants prior to heading out, the phone rang. Pete answered. After a brief conversation, Pete hung up.

"Hot damn," he said. "Guess who that was?"

"The guys who really killed Kennedy?"

Pete ignored the comment. "That was Ronald Stevens' girlfriend, Lo-retta Johnson!"

"So she knows who killed Kennedy?" said Mel.

"Will you shut up? Remember the dude that rabbited on us last week? Well, he done beat the shit out of his girlfriend and she wants to drop a dime on him." Pete was always excited about catching one that got away and had a special urge to catch up with this scumbag. It was a matter of pride.

"He's hiding out at his uncle's house on Seventy-eighth Street. Here's the setup. We head down there and find a phone booth close to the uncle's house. Then we call Lo-retta. She calls the dude to see if he's there. If he is, she calls us back, and we roll in for the bust."

The two cops headed for Seventy-seventh Division. They drove by the location on Seventy-eighth Street and stopped at a phone booth a block away on the corner at Vermont. Pete got on the phone and called the snitch. He spoke briefly and hung up.

"She's calling him now." Pete's adrenaline started to pump. *Come on*, he thought impatiently. The pay phone rang, and Pete grabbed it.

"All right," he said, "We're on our way." He hung up the phone.

"He's there! Let's go." They jumped in the car and raced the short distance down the street. Less than one minute had passed since the phone call and Pete knew Ronald couldn't move that fast, even if he knew the cops were headed his way. They jumped out of the car in front of the old single-story home.

"It's your turn to hit the front," Pete said as he headed around the side of the house toward the back yard. Pete hoped the man would try to get out the back. He'd love it if he did. It was a matter of pride.

Mel was at the front door and Pete heard him yelling for the suspect to open the door. After about a minute, Mel threatened to kick the door in. No response from inside. Not even a sound. *Thump! Thump!* Mel was kicking the door. *Thump! THUMP! How many times is he going to kick it?* wondered Pete. *Crunch! Must have been the door,* he thought. After a few agonizing seconds, the back door opened and Mel motioned Pete in.

"See anything?" asked Pete impatiently.

"Nothing." They started to search, knowing they had good probable cause. In the bedroom, they found the phone lying on the bed. The sheets were still warm. The closet . . .

"Come out of there, dipshit. You're under arrest," said Pete as he saw the suspect's feet protruding from behind the hanging clothes in the closet. The deadbeat came out with his hands up, seeing the cops with their guns pointed at the closet.

"How you pigs find me?"

"We know everything. We see all, hear all, and don't ever run from the pol-lice again!" Pete slammed the dude down on the bed and handcuffed him.

"If you ever run from me again, you'll get your ass whupped big time! Understand?"

As the cops led the suspect out the front door, Pete looked in wonder at the damage Mel had done.

"What the hell did you do to the door, Melvin?" Not only was the door off the hinges, the whole doorjamb and a large piece of plaster had come off the wall!

"He had the dead bolt on, and I had to kick it real hard to get it down," said Mel sheepishly. Pete laughed and placed one of his business cards on the table next to the shattered door. This was standard procedure when damage was done to private property in the line of duty. As long as the action was justified, the officers and the city would not be held liable for the damage. The courts had reasoned that the suspect, in such a case, should have opened the door.

A good neighbor who had come over to see what was causing all the uproar agreed to secure the premises for the uncle. The suspect was booked at the Central Jail and the cops returned to the office to do the appropriate reports about the property damage that were needed to cover their asses.

Pete felt great as he wrapped up the arrest. It had always felt good to put someone in jail that really belonged there. Two weeks later, another warrant came though the system for Ronald Stevens. He'd jumped bail again! His uncle had also notified the department that he was suing for damage to his door!

Pete was somewhat disappointed in himself for not being able to keep up with the pace that Bill Haymes had set in the construction of their gyrocopters. But he found an easy way to rationalized it: since the tools and the workshop were located in Bill's garage, that was a good enough excuse. Bill enjoyed working in the shop in his spare time. Pete's idea of after-work relaxation did not include more work.

"I should be ready to fly the glider in a couple of weeks when the glue dries on the rotor blades," advised Bill during a visit from Pete.

Pete's imagination took off when he heard the words "when the glue dries." It reminded him of Noel's warning: "What goes up, must come down." He started to think. Do I really want to go up in the air with things that are glued together? His enthusiasm for the project began to wane rapidly. Soon it was time to "test" the glider in the desert.

"Okay," said Bill as he hooked the steel tow cable to the trailer hitch on the rear of his car.

"When we get into the air, watch for our hand signals. Remember, thumbs up means *speed up* and thumbs down means *slow down*, right?" The two officers' wives sat in the convertible and looked at their husbands with a blank stare that scared the hell out of Pete!

The dry lake at El Mirage was cool and fresh in the morning, just as Pete remembered it from the times he and his buddies had ridden motorcycles there in the past. Conditions seemed perfect: the surface of the lake was smooth and dry, and there was only a slight breeze. Nothing to worry about. Nothing to worry about? Pete realized he was about to sit in a two-seater lawn chair attached to an aluminum frame that would be held aloft by wooden rotor blades *glued* together by his partner in his garage! *What's wrong with this picture?* he asked himself.

Bill finished hooking up the tow cable to the car and started to get into the lawn chair.

"Are you coming?"

"No. I just wet my pants," said Pete in a weak voice. He knew he couldn't chicken out at this late juncture, so he got into the double-wide lawn chair beside his partner.

Noel was sitting in the back seat of the convertible, checking out the movie camera she held. *This should make great film for our grandchildren*, he thought. He could hear the voice now. "Come on, kids. Let's watch Grandpa die in the movie." *Oh well*, he thought and strapped himself in.

As the car towing the gyrocopter started to pick up speed, the rotors turned faster and faster. Then the little craft literally jumped into the air! Up they went until they reached the end of the seventy-five-foot cable. As the speed of the car increased, the stress on the cable also increased. The lift created by the rotor blades Bill had glued was very efficient. The problem was there was too much lift! They had to slow down. *It was like towing a boat with a submarine*, thought Pete. The sub was too far down for the boat. The car was going too fast, and the cable was holding the aircraft down.

The stress on the cable increased, and the gyrocopter started to shake. Pete frantically gave a *thumbs-down* so the car would slow down and take the pressure off the cable before the whole 'copter disintegrated. If that happened, Pete and Bill would fall seventy-five feet to the hard surface of the dry lake.

It didn't seem to Pete that the car was slowing down. *Wasn't Noel relaying the signals to Bill's wife, Joan? Doesn't she see we are about to die? Why is she still taking movies of us while we are about to die?* All these questions blew through Pete's mind as his anger grew. He really didn't want to die this way. In a crazy contraption made by his partner. He told himself, *If I live through this, I'm gonna punch my wife out!* All the while, Pete frantically signaled for the wives to slow down.

Finally, the car started to slow. Now the gyro plummeted toward the earth. *Shit*, thought Pete, *this is it*. At the last possible second, Bill pulled the little craft up, and they bounced several times before coming to a stop. Pete unbuckled his safety belt and ran toward the car, where his wife and her friend were smiling. Pete resisted the urge to hit the smiling face.

"Didn't you see we were in trouble? Didn't you see the hand signals? We almost died!" he yelled as he waved his arms around in the air.

"I passed every command on to Joan," said Noel with a hurt in her voice.

"We did everything you told us to do." Bill's wife nodded her head in agreement.

"Okay," said Pete, "we'll wait until we get the film developed to see. But if it shows we were about to die, I'm punchin' you out."

By the time the film was ready, the whole thing seemed like a joke and was sloughed off.

Pete sold his half-finished machine to a fireman he knew. *Anyone who would be a fireman must not be too smart anyway*, reasoned Pete.

Chapter Fourteen

Julio Rivera and his friend, Sapo, watched the small drunken Latino man staggering down the street toward his home in a seedy apartment building near Pico Boulevard. Not far away was the rushing traffic of one of the busiest freeways in the world, the Santa Monica Freeway, where heavy traffic never lets up. Even though it was about eleven thirty at night, the constant roar continued. Nearby residents get used to hearing it and probably aren't even aware of it after a while.

The area where Julio and Sapo had chosen for this night's "bank withdrawal" was only about a half mile from Julio's own apartment off Seventh Street on Bixel managed by Mrs. Bordeaux. The two areas were similar in many respects. They were both in the downtown area called the Central Traffic District by the LAPD, and the population of both was about 90 percent Hispanics. Immigrants, many of them illegal, from all parts of Mexico and Central America had come to Los Angeles for various reasons. Mostly to survive. Julio had come to work but found it easier to steal.

Sapo, "the Toad," as Julio called his friend, had come to the United States as a child from Guadalajara. They shared a common dislike. They both hated people from Central America, especially Salvadorans. "*Pinche Indios,*" Julio called them. He hated them for the same reasons some people in the United States hate each other. Their accent. Their customs. Their history. Anything that was different about them. Julio never could understand why Americans didn't understand racial hatred among Latinos. He guessed it was because the Gringos thought all Latinos were Mexicans. Julio hated the Gringos for that too. In fact, there were very few people Julio did like! Sapo was just a dumb sidekick who would do anything Julio told him and would never blow the whistle to the cops if he were caught. Sapo knew what Julio would do to him if he did.

As the short dark man staggered down Pico toward the corner where Julio and Sapo were standing, Julio spoke quietly to his companion in Spanish.

"That's the guy we saw in the bar with his paycheck money. *Pinche Indio,*" he cursed.

"We'll take care of him," growled Julio under his breath. Sapo nodded as his beady eyes watched the victim walking into the spider's web.

"*Oye, hombre. Tienes un cigarillo?*" asked Julio. The smallish dark man looked up and instantly knew he was in trouble. But before he could run, the Toad jumped him. Sapo's job was to get the victim under control so that Julio could do what he loved to do. Beat his victims as a prelude to robbing them of their cash.

Julio swore as he dropped the first blow into the helpless "*Indio's*" midsection. This was his time. He was king and no one could stop him! After taking the man's money, they left him moaning and bleeding on the sidewalk. The two strong-arm robbers ran to Julio's car and sped away toward their next victim of the night.

The *Indios,* Spanish for the Native Indians in Mexico, were not the only ones Julio disliked. He especially hated the apartment manager, Mrs. Bordeaux. *She ran the apartment house like a prison,* Julio thought. Too many rules! No visitors after 10:00 p.m. No hanging around in front of the building. No loud music. On top of all that, she was French. Julio hated French people too.

In reality, Mrs. Bordeaux was Canadian. She had grown up in her native province, Quebec, where the official language is French, unlike the rest of English-speaking Canada. She had come to the United States many years before with her young son, who was partially deaf and slightly retarded, to get away from an abusive marriage. She had fought a hard battle with poverty and had taken a job as manager of the apartment she had lived in for a year or so. The apartment's owner, a wealthy car dealer, liked what she had done to make the run-down apartment pay off and had given her responsibility for his two other apartment buildings on the same block.

She had done well for herself and her son, Paul, who was now in his early thirties and still lived with her. Paul was one of the reasons Julio had let the "*Bruja Vieja*" get away with pushing him around. Julio secretly feared Bordeaux's son. Paul was short and stocky and looked like he could take care of himself in a fight. His arms were thick and hard from working on the docks of the produce market downtown. No, Julio stayed clear of Paul and cursed the old woman but stayed at the Bixel apartment. It was his headquarters, if nothing else.

Chapter Fifteen

Pete walked out of the PAB and into the officer's parking area to get his motorcycle and head for home. He pulled out onto the street that leads to the Santa Ana Freeway on-ramp at Vignes Street. As he rode north toward Vignes, he observed a car approaching the stop sign that controlled the east and west traffic. Pete had no stop sign in his direction of travel, but he instinctively slowed as he saw the car approaching the stop sign west bound. As Pete approached the intersection, the westbound car ran the stop sign and turned north in front of Pete. Pete was forced to brake and slow to avoid a possible collision. He honked his horn at the violating vehicle.

The car in front of Pete entered the freeway and moved onto the second lane. Pete pulled along the right side of the vehicle and looked at the driver. He was a young male Hispanic about twenty years old or so. The driver looked back at Pete and then, without warning, swerved to his right at Pete's motorcycle. At this point, Pete was trapped with little room to spare between the car and the railing of the bridge over the LA River. The riverbed was a good fifty feet down to the concrete below!

Pete's heart raced, and he pulled back quickly to avoid hitting the guard railing. *Damn*, he thought. *Here we go again with people trying to kill me!* He decided to take action and pulled around to the left side of the offending vehicle. The driver's window was open.

"Police!" yelled Pete. "Pull over!" The car again swerved at him. Pete waited until the man, now facing assault violations, got to the transition road to the San Bernardino Freeway, where there was a high dirt cliff area as a background and Pete fired a shot at the left rear tire. The car went about a half mile farther with Pete following behind and turned off the freeway into a bad neighborhood of East Los Angeles.

As Pete got off of his motorcycle with gun in hand, the suspect got out of his car and faced Pete.

"Go ahead! Shoot me!" he yelled. His fists were clenched and his eyes were ablaze with hatred. "Come on, Cop, shoot me!" he yelled again. Now Pete was in a bad situation in enemy territory and couldn't obviously shoot the man, who was unarmed and not attacking. Pete told the man that if he made a move toward him, he would get shot. It was a standoff!

Pete knew the only way out of this was to convince the man to give him his license information and let him go. Pete could then file a complaint the next day with the DA's Office. As Pete talked to the man, he seemed to calm down a little, so Pete could reason with him. He finally convinced the man to show his ID, and Pete wrote notes in his notebook and released the man.

A few hours after Pete arrived home, the phone rang. It was Internal Affairs.

"Were you involved in a shooting incident today?" asked the sergeant on the other end of the line.

"Yes," said Pete and related the incident and told the officer that there were no injuries or altercations and that he had intended to report it the next day.

"Get your ass down here now!" ordered the officer.

Pete complied and made the report on the department form 15.7 and retold his story to the investigators. A few days later, he was informed that the District Attorney's Office was investigating his case of use of firearms.

Not long after that, a deputy DA came to Pete's office and showed him an aerial photo of the transition road to the San Bernardino Freeway and asked Pete to identify the exact spot where he had fired his weapon. Pete told the man that he had waited until there was a high dirt wall in the direction of the shot. The DA went away.

A few weeks later, Pete was told to report to a commander's office upstairs at the PAB. He was informed that the DA's Office had turned his case back over to the department for adjudication. Pete was convinced that based on the former off-duty shooting he had been involved in, this one would also be cleared as justified.

Commander Mark Crocker had a reputation as being a no-nonsense supervisor, and Pete remembered his face from years past. Pete sat across from the commander and listened as he related the results of the investigation of Pete's off-duty shooting incident. He also repeated the policy of not shooting at moving vehicles under most circumstances.

"But, Commander, I was in fear of my life. That's why I fired at his tire to get him to stop so I could arrest him on the felony he had committed. I had to back off of the physical arrest due to my own safety hazard of being alone and in a bad area."

"You should have then tried to get his license number and a description of the suspect before using your weapon at the moving vehicle," said the commander.

"Well, sir, with all due respect, it is a little difficult to write down a license number when riding a motorcycle. And as far as describing the suspect, I think the male Hispanic, about twenty years old, would fit probably a million people in Los Angeles, don't you think?" *The handwriting was on the wall*, thought Pete and he shut up.

"I am recommending a five-day suspension in this case. The order will come down from the Chief of Police in due time." There it was! Pete's first suspension of his career as a cop!

"Wow, Pete," said Mel later. "I'm sorry to hear that."

"You know, I really don't give a shit because I was right and my life was protected, and so I can deal with it. Besides, all it means is that I lose a week's pay and have to work five more days before I can retire!"

A warm LA spring breeze was blowing away the smog today. It made it almost bearable to be driving in the streets of urban Los Angeles. Mel was on a day off, and Pete was enjoying the drive as he turned the plain-colored car onto Eagle Rock Boulevard and headed into Highland Park Division. Sherry Barone had gotten out of jail after doing her ninety days and had called Pete. She was going to take Pete up on the offer he had made to help her out in getting her job back. Pete still felt a twinge of guilt at having turned her in to Accident Investigation Follow-up and sending her to jail. *Oh well*, he told himself for the twentieth time, *it was the best thing to do.*

Pete was familiar with the neighborhood, having spent many days patrolling Highland Park as a motor cop. That's how he had met Sherry's mother. She had worked in the bowling alley on Eagle Rock Boulevard. Pete put those reminiscences out of his mind. He didn't want to think about past mistakes now. And he didn't want to make another one with her daughter, Sherry.

He knew she and her sister had moved back in with her grandfather, and he knew both of them were taking advantage of the old man. *What a racket*, he thought. He guessed the old man must have some money. He also guessed that with all his wayward relatives moving in, Grandpa wouldn't have it long.

Pete pulled up in front of the old gray stucco house about a block off Eagle Rock and walked up to the door. It was open.

"Hey. Anybody home?"

"Hi," said a silhouette inside. "Come on in."

Sherry gave him a hug and asked him to sit down. Pete looked around. The house was dingy and old. It smelled old. Not dirty, just old and dingy. Pete wanted out but he listened to Sherry as she told him how she had changed and was going to stay straight and get a good job. She said all the things Pete expected to hear her say. He promised to talk to her former boss at the garment shop where she used to work when he had found her. The longer he stayed and talked to Sherry, the more nervous he got.

When he finally got out of the house and back into his car, he breathed a sigh of relief. It wasn't that he didn't want to help her out. He did. It was that uneasy feeling cops get when they know they are sticking their necks out for people involved in the criminal element. He knew Sherry had hung with hypes and suppliers. He knew she was capable of making unwise decisions like hit-and-run accidents. He had a hollow feeling in the pit of his stomach.

Pete did go to see the owner of the garment shop and was able to talk the man into giving Sherry another chance at her old job. Sherry was elated! When Pete told her on the phone, she started to cry.

"If there's anything I can do for you . . . ," her voice trailed off.

"Just stay off the shit," said Pete. After hanging up, he sat and looked at the phone for a few seconds, wondering how he'd gotten himself into this situation.

Chapter Sixteen

"Officer Felix?" asked the voice on the phone.

"This is Officer Felix."

"This is Lo-retta Johnson. Are y'all still lookin' for Ronald Stevens?"

"You bet," said Pete. Ronald had eluded Mel and Pete now for almost a year since he had jumped bail again. The lawsuit his uncle had filed because Mel had kicked down the door the last time they arrested Ronald had been thrown out of court, but Ronald was still loose on the streets.

Ronald's problem was, among many, he couldn't stay away from Lo-retta. He also couldn't stay off drugs and alcohol. When he was high, he abused women. Lo-retta was handy. She had put up with him for several months now, and last night was all she could stand. He beat her again. This time, she called the police. Not the patrol cops. The warrant cops. She knew they wanted him badly. She was right.

"Damn, Mel. I want to get that mutha real bad," Pete had groaned after the last attempt to find Ronald had failed.

"Don't take it so hard," Mel had said. "There are a lot more out there to bust. Why worry about one dude?"

"It's a matter of principle. It's like a game. And he makes fools out of us."

"The system is what makes fools out of all of us," said Mel. "There are so many holes in it for rats to run out of it's pitiful."

"I know. When I first came on the job, I couldn't believe it. Bail is supposed to make sure the defendant comes back to court. They set the amount based on the seriousness of the charge and the background of the suspect. The constitution prohibits 'excessive bail,' so at some point, the courts have ruled that a lot of people can't make bail because they're poor. What's reasonable to one person may be excessive to another. So whadda they do? They revise the bail system to let suspects post only ten percent of the full bail amount. So a person charged with, say, robbery could have bail set at ten thousand dollars and only have to come up with one thousand of it to get out of jail."

"Yeah. Then you hear on the news that a suspect gets arrested and bail is set at ten thousand dollars, but they never mention that the suspect could be on the streets by just posting a thousand," Mel chimed in.

Cops hated the bail system. They also hated the fact that the record keeping of the courts was far behind, as was also the police department's ability to check records on newly arrested people before they made bail. Many times, offenders were released on bail before it was discovered that they were wanted by other agencies or were using a phony name. Even when they used their own names, many times they slipped through the cracks!

"Working warrants is like wiping your butt with a hoop. There's no end to it!" whined Pete.

"So Ronald's girlfriend is droppin' another dime on him, huh?"

"Yep, and we're gonna put that son of a bitch in jail for good this time," bragged Pete.

"Wanna bet?" asked Melvin.

The game of hide-and-seek went into high gear. Pete dragged Mel down to the meeting place where he had arranged to meet Lo-retta. Mel was tired of this game. He couldn't see why his partner was so focused on catching this dude. Why was this particular bail-jumper so damned important? To Pete he was. He was symbolic of all the people who play that lousy game. It wasn't because Ronald was black or that his crimes were minor compared to others on the street. To Pete, it was a matter of principle.

When they reached the meeting place, Lo-retta filled them in.

"He been stayin' in an apartment on Broadway near Fifty-first Street. He don't go out much, and he don't even answer the phone. His sister live across the hall an' takes all the calls for him."

"Sounds like he's really hinky."

"He sho' is. He'll talk to me though," she said. Pete hatched an idea in his head.

"Okay, here's the deal. You follow us to the pad. You call him from a phone outside. When his sister calls him to the phone, we nail him." Mel shook his head, but he knew there was no stopping Pete now. They went to the location and found a phone booth.

"Give us a few minutes to get in place, then call him," instructed Pete.

Ronald's apartment was in the front of the building on the second floor at the top of the stairs. His sister's apartment was directly across the hall from his. Pete and Mel took up positions at the bottom of the stairs in front of the building where they could look up and see the doors to both apartments. They waited. The faint sound of a telephone rang upstairs. The door of one of the apartments opened, and a woman came out and banged on the door across the hall.

"It's dat bitch again," she yelled. The door opened and Ronald came out. Pete ran the twenty or so steps up to the second floor. He felt like he was traveling in slow motion, afraid he would lose the suspect before he got to him. Ronald's eyes recognized the two cops that dogged his life and turned back into his room. The door slammed and locked. Pete knew there was no way Ronald could get out except through the door and doubted that he would jump from a second story window. Too bad, thought Pete.

When they reached the top of the stairs there was no one in sight. The sister had run back into her apartment also. Pete lined up on Ronald's door.

"This one's mine," he said with determination in his voice. *Bam!* The door flew open and in went the two cops with guns in hand. Ronald was hiding in the closet, as usual. Pete pulled him out and smacked him alongside his head with his open hand. Ronald went down on the bed, covering up his head and yelling.

"Don't be hittin' on me, man" he wailed.

"Why not, asshole? You're always hittin' on someone else. How does it feel?" Pete handcuffed the whining suspect, and they booked him at Central Jail. A few weeks later, Mel was sorting out Greenies in the office.

"Oh, Peeeete," said Mel in the tiny voice he used to get Pete pissed off, "It's a good thing you didn't bet me that Ronald Stevens wouldn't be out again." Pete knew what Mel was about to say and held up his hand to stop him.

"It's like wiping your butt with a hoop," he said as he shook his head.

Pete and his partner prided themselves for not allowing suspects to get away from them, but the record was not perfect. One sunny afternoon, Pete was out alone in the Highland Park area with a handful of warrants. He chose one and drove to an older neighborhood with nice shade trees on both sides of the street that reminded him of Iowa and his childhood. He reminisced as he got out of his car, enjoying the clear air that sometimes makes Los Angeles a nice place to be.

The address on the warrant was a small old dwelling made of stucco and with the flat roof that seemed to be popular in the 1940s. The warrant was for a male Caucasian, thirty years old and about six feet tall. It was a minor warrant for failure to appear on a DUI case. Pete knocked on the front door. After a moment, a voice from inside asked who it was.

"Police. Open the door please." As soon as the words left Pete's mouth, he knew he had made a mistake. Then he heard loud footsteps running inside and knew the suspect was not going to open the door and was going to run!

Pete was not about to chase a suspect without a backup officer or his partner with him. He saw a small window to the left of the front door that was open. Pete looked in the window just in time to see the suspect pulling himself up into an opening in the ceiling that lead to the roof. Pete reached in the window and grabbed the man's leg and pulled down on it. The man shook his leg loose, and up he went onto the roof. Pete ran around the house, hoping to catch the man if he jumped off the roof. The drop was only about eight or nine feet. From the other side of the house he heard a *thud* and ran in that direction to try and catch the man. By the time Pete arrived, he saw the man running down the street and had a good lead on Pete.

Pete could have called in patrol cops to search the area, but he said to himself, "Why ruin a nice day looking for some dipshit for DUI." He returned to the front door and left a notice and logged it as a due diligence stop.

Chapter Seventeen

"What are the coveralls for?" asked Mel as he watched Pete loading them into the trunk of the police vehicle. Then Pete produced a large package wrapped in brown paper and tied with string. He put it into the trunk also.

"What the hell was that?" asked Mel with a look of disbelief.

"That, my friend, is my secret weapon."

"Weapon? What kind of a weapon? We've got enough weapons now we can't use."

"I've been thinking of a way to catch these turkeys we play hide-and-seek with. Most of them are at work during the day, or they won't come to the door when we show up at their pads. You know Leroy's mama ain't gonna give his skinny ass up to the po-lice no way. I thought we'd take a different approach." The two cops got into the car and headed out toward Seventy-seventh Division.

"I put together a list of several dudes we've checked on before, and were told they weren't home or they were at work. Enough time has gone by that I don't think they will recognize me in my outfit."

"What outfit?" asked Mel, not really wanting to hear this.

"I'm gonna dress up like a delivery man with a package for the suspect. I'm gonna tell the person at the door that the package must be delivered to the party in person. I've even made up a bunch of labels with their names on them to stick on the package. They won't be able to resist picking up the package." Pete smiled with self-pride at his great idea. He looked at Mel, waiting for his approval. There was a long pause.

"Are you nuts?" said Mel. Pete's ego dropped on the floor.

"What makes you think the Department is going to go for this?"

"Why not? Do they want us to arrest these people or not? What's wrong with a little trick to catch a crook?" Pete's logic seemed right to him.

"It'll never work," scoffed Mel. "But hey, don't let me stop you."

"You just wait and see," said Pete with his nose up in the air.

They stopped about a half block from the house of a warrant suspect. Pete got out and opened the trunk. He slipped into the coveralls and messed up his hair before donning the baseball cap. His dark glasses covered his eyes. He took a clipboard, a pen, and the package and started off toward the house. Mel stayed in the car, shaking his head as he watched his partner.

"What choo wont?" came the answer from the woman at the door.

"Special delivery for Antoine Jefferson, ma'am."

"He ain't here. I'll sign fo' it."

"Sorry, ma'am, I can only deliver it to the person named on the package. I don't make the rules." Pete stepped back a half step, letting her see the label but holding tight to the package.

"Wha's in it?" asked the woman.

"I have no idea. But it's insured, so it must be valuable." Pete watched as the woman thought.

"Antoine at work but he be back about three o'clock."

"Well, I'll try to come back then, but if he's not here, the package goes in the dead-mail bin."

"The 'dead-mail bin'?" she repeated.

"The dead-mail bin," Pete said again.

"You come back an' he be here," promised the woman. Pete left and walked back to the car. Mel was still shaking his head. The two cops returned to the address at three fifteen that afternoon. Antoine Jefferson was there waiting for his special delivery.

"Oh man, dat ain't fair," whined Antoine as Pete put the handcuffs on him. "You po-lice ain't s'posed to lie."

"Why not? You lied when you promised to appear on that drunk-driving charge, didn't you?"

"Tha's different, man. I mean, if you can't trust the cops, who can you trust, man?"

"Life's a bitch, ain't it?"

Mel couldn't believe his eyes! The trick worked several more times, and Pete was booking nearly everyone of the people he pulled the "special delivery" trick on. That is until Pete's captain heard about it. Pete was summoned before his commander.

"What the hell are you doing, Felix? What is this package-delivery crap you've been pulling?" The captain's voice was high-pitched and agitated. Captain Coy was an old-timer, who Pete had judged, was marking time in R&I until he was ready to retire. He didn't want anyone to make waves on his little lake.

"Well, Captain, I thought I was doing my job. You know, it gets tiresome having people tell you a suspect isn't home when you know they are probably layin' up in the bed while you're talking to they momma at the door," said Pete with sarcasm in his voice. He knew what was about to happen.

"You will stop this package thing immediately. I'll be considering what, if any, action I may take against you."

"How about a class B commendation?" suggested Pete. The captain's face flushed another shade of red.

"Get the fuck out of here!" he yelled. The "package scam," as it was called by the men in the detail, came to an end. The legend went on, however.

Pete and Mel received a request from the Martinez, CA Police Department to pick up a person they had arrested on an LA warrant in their city. The man had been in custody for two days, and he needed to be transported to Los Angeles before the five-day limit statute on misdemeanor warrants ran out.

"Well, I hate these little jaunts around the state to pick up these crooks," whined Pete as he and Mel checked out a "cage-car" with a screen between the front and back seat for carrying prisoners. It was six o'clock in the morning, and Pete was in a bad mood. Mel was in his bright, shiny health nut glory.

"You should get up this early every morning and run a couple of miles before breakfast." Mel had that little smirk on his face knowing his comment would get Pete's goat.

"Even if you came to my house and put your gun to my head and told me to get up and do that, I would have to really think about what would be worse, getting shot or getting up!" Mel giggled knowing that as soon as they got on the road to drive to Martinez, Pete would be fast asleep anyway.

The drive to Martinez was about 370 miles one way, and the department frowned on cops staying overnight if at all possible, so they were under orders to make the round trip in one day. That would be a long day for the guys but Pete knew that Mel liked to drive so he could nap most of the way.

On arrival at the Martinez jail about noon, the Martinez jail officer brought out the arrestee.

"Holy Moly," cried Pete, "it's Jesus!" The young man was dressed in a gown or smock from head to foot. He also had a beard and hair down to his shoulders. The man was involved in some weird cult of some kind, the guys guessed. They signed all the paperwork and quickly hustled the weirdo dude to the police car. Pete removed the handcuffs from the prisoner in compliance with policy when driving cross-country with a prisoner. With a metal cage between the back and front seats, there was no danger from the prisoner. There was also a rule that allowed prisoners to refuse to fly if they didn't want to travel in that mode.

When the two cops and the arrestee got on the freeway south toward home, Pete noticed a foul odor in the car.

"Hey, Partner, did you forget to bathe this morning or has your deodorant let you down?" asked Pete with a frown on his face and his fingers holding his nose.

"It's not me!"

"Then it must be Creepy Jesus back there. Hey, when was the last time you took a bath, man?"

"The body doesn't need baths. If you smell, you smell. It's God's will," answered their passenger.

"Well, I can't take this shit all the way to LA. Mel, pull over at the next convenience store."

A few miles later, they stopped and Pete went into the store. Pete returned shortly with a spray can of Right Guard deodorant.

"Step out here, Skunk Boy, and pull up your dress!" commanded Pete as he shook the spray can. When the prisoner pulled up his shroud, Pete sprayed him up and down and under his arms with deodorant. The prisoner was back in the car, and they were off in a flash.

"Now don't you feel better, Brother John?" asked Pete through the wire screen.

"Damn, you smell good now. I wonder if Right Guard could use this in a commercial." Mel just shook his head and drove on.

Chapter Eighteen

"Pete. It's for you," said Billy Much as he handed over the phone. Pete had just come in and hadn't even had time to get his first cup of coffee and was not in the mood for early morning phone calls.

"Shit! Can't they see I'm busy?" he grumbled.

"This is Officer Felix. Oh, hello, Mrs. Bordeaux. How are you? What? Sure, but . . . ah . . . we'll see you in an hour or so."

"What's that all about?" asked Mel.

"I don't really know. She said it's very important that she see us and give us some papers. That's all she would say on the phone."

"Don't forget, we've got that funeral to go to today, Partner," reminded Mel. One of the cops in the Valley had died in a traffic accident, and his funeral was set for 11:00 a.m. that day.

"Damn it. Yeah, I had forgotten about that. We can go see the old lady first and then head out to the Valley." They finished their office work and headed out for Bixel Street.

Pete had gotten to know Mrs. Bordeaux over the past few months. He and Mel had attempted to serve several warrants in the apartment houses she managed. On one visit, when Mel was off, she gave Pete a small old desk that she had taken from one of her apartments due to a burn spot on the writing area. Pete's wife had refinished the desk, and it now resided in their bedroom. Pete liked the old lady and admired her strength and her bravery to stand up to some of her worst tenants.

As the two officers pulled up in front of the building entrance where Mrs. Bordeaux lived, they didn't have time to get out of the car before the small blond woman came quickly to the car. She appeared very agitated.

"Please, may I get in zee car?"

"Sure, hop in the back," said Pete, wondering what could be so important.

"Please take thees letter and eef anything happen to me, you weel know why." She was tense and anxious as she spoke. Pete opened the envelope and pulled out several handwritten pages of yellow notepaper.

"You read it now, eh?" she pleaded. Pete read aloud so Mel could hear too.

The letter related how Mrs. Bordeaux had given Julio Rivera an eviction notice and told him he would have to move because of his abuse of his wife and his failure to comply with house rules. Julio had become angry and threatened her. The next day, while she and another Latino tenant were painting a vacant apartment, Julio came into the room and pulled out a large hunting knife. He then put the knife against the woman's belly and said he was going to kill her.

The Canadian told him, in no uncertain terms, that she was not afraid of him and for him to go ahead and kill her. When he backed down, she and the other tenant tried to leave the room. Julio again threatened them with the knife and would not let them leave the apartment for another thirty minutes or so.

"Damn, Partner. If this is true, we've got an assault with a deadly weapon and a technical kidnapping on two victims!" exclaimed Pete. Both cops knew that the legal definition of kidnapping also included keeping a person from leaving a location by the use of force or fear. Technically, Julio had committed a kidnap on the two people in the apartment when he held then there at knifepoint, not allowing them to leave.

"Eeet ees all true. I 'ave weetness too. One beeg man who live in apartments see everything. He ees tell that peeg to leave us alone, and then Julio, he chase heem with the knife too! I tell you thees so eef I die, you know who ees keel me."

"Don't worry, Mrs. Bordeaux, he ain't gonna hurt anyone. We'll see to that. Is he up there now?"

"He ees not home now. I see heem go out thees morning, and he ees not come back yet."

"How about letting us use your phone?"

"You come."

"I'm going to call a radio car to take the crime report, and we'll stick around for a little while, but we have to go to an officer's funeral out in the San Fernando Valley at eleven."

"Don't worry about me. I take care of myself, Pete. You go."

Pete called Rampart Station and requested a radio car to come and take a crime report.

"We'll come back after the funeral and check on you, okay?" said Mel.

It was about three o'clock when they returned to the Bixel apartment house. Mrs. Bordeaux met them at the door of her apartment.

"Everytheen ees fine. The police come and make report and then take heem away."

"That's great," said Pete. "What's the name of the other man you said tried to help you and was threatened by Rivera? We want to talk to him."

"Hee's name ees Joe Palmer. Hee's work at the tattoo parlor down on Third and Main."

Pete and Mel pulled up in front of the tattoo parlor where the third victim worked.

"How about a tattoo of a puppy on your arm, Melvin. Or a carrot maybe?"

"How about if I tattoo your head bone with my baton, sweetie?" retorted Mel.

The tattoo guy was just what you'd expect. Big belly, long hair, and beard and . . . tattoos! He was more than willing to talk to the cops.

"Jesus, the guy is a nutcase! He comes after me with this big hunting knife, so I jump in my car and split. He jumps in his car and chases me around town. I think he had a gun in the car. Anyway, I was scared shitless!" The cops listened intently.

"So I'm drivin' around hoping to see a cop car, and there was one, stopped near Figueroa Street. So I come screechin' to a stop behind 'em and jump out. This Rivera guy stops just down the street. So I yell to the cops, 'That guy in that car is trying to kill me. He's got a knife and maybe a gun in the car. What do the cops do? They search me! They find a joint in one of my pockets, and I go to jail for possession! They didn't even check out the other car, and this asshole skates while I hit the slammer!"

By this time, the two partners are numb. Pete is thinking that it doesn't surprise him with today's "new breed of cop." After getting a statement, they leave, telling the tattoo guy not to worry; they'll straighten out everything. They headed back over to Bixel to talk to Mrs. Bordeaux again. When they arrive, she is near hysteria.

"Oh my God. Eee's back and ees knife too," she wails.

"What? I thought you said they arrested him," said Pete.

"They deed but ees back and ees got the knife again. I see heem under my window looking at me."

"This is crazy," said Pete. "I'm going over to Rampart Station and see what the hell's going on. Mel, will you stay here and hang till I get back?"

Mel agreed and Pete headed for the Rampart Station with a vengeance.

He stormed into the Detective Bureau and confronted the sergeant behind the desk. As Pete started to talk, he noticed the sergeant look at the ID card fastened to his jacket to see what Pete's rank was.

"Patrol took the report and brought the guy in, and we determined it to be a misdemeanor and took a battery report," said the detective with a sneer on his lips.

"Battery my ass! That was two good ADWs and a technical kidnapping. Any of those should have put this asshole in the slammer, but you guys give him back his knife and send him out the door? I can't believe what I'm hearing!" The conversation stormed back and forth for several minutes, then Pete made a suggestion.

"Look, I'll call this woman on the phone and I won't tell her you're listening and I'll have her tell her story for me again. You listen and tell me what you think then."

The detective reluctantly agreed, and Pete got Mrs. Bordeaux on the line. As she unfolded her story again, the detective's face got redder and redder. When Pete hung up the phone, the detective coughed and cleared his throat.

"I'll have that report changed to reflect her charges right away," he said. Pete thanked him and left.

When he arrived back at the apartment house, he pulled his partner aside.

"What the hell's happening to this department? First, the patrol cops take two serious felonies and report them as misdemeanors, and then they turn the armed suspect loose, with his knife, to threaten the victims again! Another victim runs to the cops for help, and they put *him* in jail for having one stinking joint in his pocket and don't even question the real bad guy! I can't believe my ears!" Pete was livid.

"What are we gonna do about it, Pete? We've done all we can do, haven't we?"

"What if this asshole kills the old lady? How will we feel then?" Pete grew quiet for a moment then spoke to his partner.

"Here's the deal. This guy doesn't understand anything but force. He's not afraid of the cops because they don't do anything to him! I'm gonna get his attention."

"How're ya gonna do that, Pete?"

"The 'old-fashioned way.' Up close and personal. Look, Mel, you don't have to go with me if you don't want to, but I'm not gonna stand by and let the LAPD screw up and get this nice lady killed 'cause nobody gives a shit! But I don't want to get you in trouble either. You've got a few more years to go for your twenty. I've got mine."

Mel thought for a minute and then said, "I'm with you." They went upstairs to the third floor and walked softly down to the suspect's apartment.

"Let me handle this," said Pete. He knocked on the door. The door opened and the big Latino stood there.

"Wha' you wan'?"

"You Julio Rivera?" asked Pete.

"Yeah. Wha' you wan', man?"

"Police. Step out here into the hallway. We want to talk to you."

Julio moved into the hall and closed the door to his apartment. Pete's right arm flashed out. He aimed the open-handed blow to the left side of the man's face. The blow landed with a loud slap! Julio slid down the wall to a sitting position with a groan. Pete pulled him to his feet by the shirt.

"Listen you *hijo de su chingada madre*, if anything happens to Mrs. Bordeaux or anyone else in this building, I'll kill you myself. Do you understand, asshole?" Pete was in the guy's face, speaking in a low, tight voice, his teeth clenched together.

"You've been told to move out of this building, and an eviction notice has been served. If I were you, I'd get my ass out of town and back to Mexico, or wherever you crawled in from. Do you hear me, *cabrone?*"

Julio just nodded his head to indicate his understanding. At that time, his wife opened the door and stuck out her head.

"Qué pasó aqui?"

"Nada mas," said Pete as he turned and walked back down the hall with Mel following.

Before the day was over, they got a radio call to phone the station.

Chapter Nineteen

"Damn, Pete. I just overheard a call come in complaining about you guys beating someone up," said Billy Much. Billy was working light duty after an off-duty sport accident and was working the desk in the office until he was fit for duty again. "I thought you guys would like to know. Does it ring any bells?"

"Yeah, it does, Billy. Thanks for the heads-up call." Pete hung up the phone and turned to his partner.

"Well, it didn't take that rotten son of a bitch long to blow the whistle on us, Mel."

"Was that about Rivera?" Pete nodded, and Mel shook his head in disgust.

"What are we gonna do?"

"Look, Partner, I said I didn't want to get you in trouble and I meant it. Here's what I think: I told you that I'm on my way out. I know I can't do this job anymore the way things are. Cops don't want to do police work. The guys in our unit won't even listen to the radio calls. The department won't back us. The Rampart cops are idiots. Some of the patrol cops can't even make a decent arrest. So there are two choices, it seems to me. One is we lie and say we didn't do anything more than shove the guy up against the wall and let them take their best shot at us. Which means me *and* you. Or two, I'll cop out and say you weren't there or you tried to stop me but I wouldn't listen. I'll get some time off, but what the fuck, I don't really care anymore. You'll probably get a little reprimand for being dumb enough to work with me." Mel put his head down in thought. Pete had to say one more thing.

"Let's think about this for a minute. Who are the bad guys here? Who's trying to do the right thing and protect and serve like the slogan says on our cars? Has the department protected Mrs. Bordeaux and her tenants? Who patted the bad guy on the wrist, then handed him back his knife and kicked him back out onto the streets? Who're wearing the white hats here? Are we gonna let some fucking illegal alien who beats his wife and threatens people's lives beat us?" He paused and took a deep breath. "But it's your choice, and I'll abide by it without any bad feeling for you, Partner. You tell me what to do."

There was a long silence while they thought. Then Mel looked up.

"Fuck 'em! You're right! We are the good guys! Let 'em take their best shot!" The two partners shook hands and prepared for the fight ahead.

Internal Affairs Division, or IAD, has a necessary function for police departments. Pete had only been there once. That was the time he had been a little rough with a juvenile arrest and was charged with an excessive force complaint. In that case, the charges were false and he was cleared, but it still scared the hell out of him. This case was different. The world was different. The department was different. How? *Why were things so different?* he wondered.

He had seen the statistics on juvenile crime go sky-high in the past few years. He had seen the rise of the Civil Rights Movement, while the liberal courts in the country bent and twisted the laws, thwarting the will of the people who wanted to see criminals treated like criminals. Now it appeared that victims of crime received less consideration than the bastards who victimized them. It seemed the department had reached the point where its first priority was to be politically correct. That translated into being kinder and more sensitive in its treatment of suspects even if that meant being *less* sensitive to the rights of citizens who file complaints.

No one seemed to care about the millions of warrants that went unserved. And what about the millions of dollars in fines that never got collected? If cops spent time arresting warrant suspects, was that a bad thing? Was it better not to agitate the community by coming to a person's home and arresting him on his outstanding warrant? Why were motor cops now being discouraged from running warrant checks on people they stop for traffic violations? Bad for public relations? It appeared the game of hide-and-seek was fixed. Fixed on the side of the bad guys!

All of a sudden, he didn't care anymore. He couldn't fight the system anymore. Now the system was fighting him, and it wasn't a pleasant fight.

The LAPD Internal Affairs Division had a reputation for being very aggressive and thorough in its investigations of officers accused of misconduct. Despite what the news media has said about IAD not policing their "own," it was not true. Pete had known several officers who had been terminated or served long suspensions as a result of IAD investigations. It all stemmed from the command of former Chief William H. Parker, when he took charge of a corrupt Los Angeles City Police Department the early 1950s.

Parker, a man with a military background, wanted to clean up the department that had seen too much political involvement in the 1930s and

1940s. That had led to more vice and corruption on the streets and had developed a reputation for the LAPD as one of the rottenest police departments in the nation. Chief Parker's approach to reforming the LAPD was to turn it into a "quasi-military" organization. Strict uniform rules. Long-sleeved wool shirts. Caps had to be worn, even while driving your police vehicle! Any officer caught not wearing his cap while conducting police business was subject to reprimand.

Moral turpitude rules were strict. Any officer caught cohabitating with a person not their spouse was terminated. It was forbidden to allow a police contact to turn into personal relationship. Officers' homes were expected to be well maintained and look neat. Pete knew one officer who had received a call from his supervisor advising him that a neighbor had complained about the officer's lawn not being kept up. The officer was ordered to mow his lawn! Pete remembered hearing the instructors tell the cadets in training that "If you don't like the rules, go pump gas or sell shoes for a living!" Anyone wanting to become an officer under the leadership of Chief Parker had to have a strong dedication to the job.

When Chief Parker died in 1966, the department underwent sweeping changes. Many were good, but discipline among the troops was less military. Still, IAD could strike fear into the hearts of most officers.

Pete's first meeting with IAD was not as bad as he had expected. Partly because he knew that Julio Rivera had run back to Mexico and wouldn't be testifying against him. But there was still a chance that IAD would try to bring Pete down.

"Officer Felix, I'm Sergeant Renaldo and this is Sergeant McKinney. We are the investigating officers on this case." Pete shook hands with them. The two sergeants were younger than Pete and that was cause for a little worry. Some young officers, when put in positions that carried a little power, had been known to use that power, trying to advance themselves on the department. Pete sat down behind a table. He noticed a tape recorder in front of him was in operation.

"Do you have any objections to being recorded?"

"No." Pete was going to take the approach that he had nothing to hide.

After being advised of his Miranda Rights, the interview began. Pete had made a written statement several weeks ago, right after he was advised of the charges against him. The investigators would be looking for any changes in his story. Pete laid out the chain of events leading up to the confrontation with Rivera. He stuck to his story that he had only shoved Rivera against the wall. He admitted threatening him against harming the apartment manager, Mrs. Bordeaux.

"Have you interviewed Mr. Rivera?" asked Pete, knowing they had not.

"Not as yet," said Renaldo. They obviously didn't know that Pete knew he wasn't around to be interviewed.

"Officer Felix, are you willing to take a lie detector test?"

"Wheel it out," he said with a wave of his hand.

There was a short period of silence, and then Sergeant Renaldo spoke.

"Excuse us for a moment." The investigators stepped into another office. After a few minutes, they returned.

"Say, did that sergeant at Rampart ever change that crime report from a misdemeanor to a felony, as he said he would?" asked Pete.

"The report is still for a misdemeanor complaint," answered the IAD Investigator.

"That rotten son of a bitch," Pete cursed.

"You may go now. We may want to talk to you again. Thanks."

"No problem," said Pete, putting on a friendly smile. As he left the fifth floor of the police building, he breathed a sigh of relief. It wasn't over yet, but things were looking up.

The next day, Mel had his turn in the barrel. Later, Pete and his partner compared notes. Mel and Pete had told the same story, most of which was true, all except for the use of force part.

"Those IAD guys sure have a hard job," Mel commented as they walked to their car to hit the road.

"Yeah, but they'll try to fake us out and trip us up, so let's not discuss it any more until we hear something. I wouldn't put it past them to bug our vehicle. It's been done before. You ever hear the story about the officer that offered his partner a hotdog from his lunch? The car was bugged and one of the officers knew it. So the conversation went something like this:

"Hey, Partner, you like weenies? Here, try one of mine."

The other officer quickly replied, "Say *hotdog*, say *hotdog*!"

Mel looked at his partner with a blank look.

"Don't you get it?" asked Pete.

"I don't think it's funny."

"Damn, it's tough working with a partner that doesn't have a sense of humor," said Pete, shaking his head.

Chapter Twenty

IAD's investigation lasted several months. The two partners waited for the outcome. They were not suspended while the investigation dragged on, and it was hard to work while the pressure was on from IAD, but they did their job like always, putting the bad guys in jail.

As the time went by, there were several developments in the case. Even the fact that Julio Rivera had disappeared back to Mexico did not discourage IAD! Of course not! We don't need no stinking complaining party! The investigation rolled on.

After his little run-in with LAPD, the tattoo guy had left town too. The owner of the apartment building that Mrs. Bordeaux managed told her that he had written a letter of commendation to the department. The letter thanked Officer Felix and Officer Tennesen for "saving the life of his apartment manager." That commendation somehow "got lost" and was never heard of or seen by Pete or Mel.

Pete became more and more disheartened as the time rolled on with no report from IAD. One day, while off duty, he was shopping in a bookstore in West Los Angeles when a woman came into the store, complaining about some men who were drinking in the parking lot. They had verbally harassed her and other women passing by. Pete identified himself as a cop to the frightened woman and said he would take a look.

He walked out into the parking lot just in time to see one of the men run out into the street to say something to a woman in a car stopped at a traffic light. The woman quickly sped away, as if frightened. Pete saw there were three Caucasian men, who appeared to be laborers or contractors. They wore work clothes and were drinking beer from a case they'd stashed in the bed of a pickup truck parked in the parking lot. Realizing that several violations of the law were occurring, he went back into the bookstore.

"May I use your phone? Police business." The clerk immediately agreed.

When the desk officer at the West LA Station answered, Pete asked for the watch commander.

"Los Angeles Police Department, Sergeant Morgan," answered the phone.

"Sarge, this is Pete Felix, serial number 10166. I'm off duty, calling from a phone at . . ." Pete filled in the location and requested a patrol car and said he would back them up when the car arrived. After about five minutes, a black-and-white police car arrived. Pete went out to meet them. When the suspects saw the police car, they started to get rid of the beer in a trash can. The officers responding to the call were a male training officer and a female rookie trainee. Pete advised them to be careful, as these guys looked bad.

The patrol officers approached the suspects and began to interrogate them. Pete stood by. To his surprise, he heard the training officer tell the three men to "get out of here." The men eagerly complied and drove away in two vehicles.

"Whoa, you guys didn't even write FIs or do any record checks on those guys! Besides, they were all under the influence, and you just sent them out on the street!"

The training officer looked at Pete with a smirk. "We handled it, didn't we?"

"Both your asses would be hung if one of those cars gets in a wreck down the street. Besides, how do you know if any of them had warrants?"

The "training" officer walked back to his car, and the female rookie followed. Without another word, they drove off. Pete couldn't believe what had happened! He seethed inside at the lack of commitment the duty the officers had shown and the miserable example he had set for the rookie cop in his care. He didn't go back into the bookstore because he couldn't face the citizens he had promised to assist. He went instead to the West LA Police Station.

As he faced the day-watch commander, he tried to calm down.

"Sarge, I just came from that call I put in regarding a disturbance at the bookstore."

"Yeah, and . . . ?"

Pete related the story to the sergeant and then said, "Look, I don't want to get anybody burned, but these officers handled this incident all wrong. I think they need some special training, especially that so-called training officer!" Pete knew he was turning red in the face as his temper got hotter as he talked.

"I'll take care of it, Felix," the sergeant promised.

Pete left feeling a little better but wondering if the sergeant would keep his promise. What in hell was the department coming to? First, Rampart screws up a case that could have ended in the death of a woman, then West LA officers screw up this one!

The next day, Pete's immediate supervisor, Sergeant Wilson, called him into his office.

"What the hell do you mean by marching into the watch commander's office in West LA Division and telling them how to run their business?" the sergeant yelled.

Pete was dumbfounded. "What are you talking about?"

"The watch commander over there called and complained about your attitude and trying to burn a couple of their officers."

"My attitude? Jesus Christ! I'm out there trying to protect innocent citizens from drunken slobs and two of LA's finest come out and screw it up! They deserved to get burned for what they did, or didn't do, but I didn't ask for that! I just said they needed training!" *This is all I need*, thought Pete.

"You write me up however you want, Sarge. I really don't give a shit!" He stomped out of the sergeant's office and went back to work.

Pete went to visit one of his old friends to try and relax a bit with an old friend. They were sitting on Bill's front porch, smoking a good cigar and having a beer, talking about old times. One of Bill's neighbors saw the two sitting on the porch and came over to join them. Pete had met Bill's neighbor briefly before but never had a conversation with him.

"You're the LA cop, right?" asked the man.

"Yep," said Pete, "at least for a while anyway. I'm getting close to retirement time."

"How long have you been a cop now?"

"Coming up on twenty-three years now."

"What's it like? I mean, really? I imagine it changes your way of thinking. Pete hesitated to answer and then did anyway. Bill smiled.

"Well, since you asked, being a cop and dealing with the law and the judicial system makes you start thinking in a more legalistic way. You're right. You start to change, at least in the eyes of others. It makes it harder to communicate."

"In what way?" asked the man leaning forward in his chair.

"You develop a different attitude and approach to things from being a cop. I'm not saying it's a bad change. From others' points of view, it may seem to be, but the changes are necessary ones to a cop. Without them, he can't survive." Pete puffed on his cigar and blew smoke up toward the sky.

"You have to be firm, but fair. You gotta be ready to use force when it is required and you can't lose! If you lose you may be dead."

"Wow! Sounds pretty scary to me." Pete nodded in agreement.

"It changes you."

Bill's neighbor seemed mesmerized by now.

"Do the effects of these experiences begin to show up in your personality?"

"Good question," commended Pete. "You realize one day that you can't change the world. You can't even change people. You have to deal with the world the way it is and accept it the way it is or you will be overcome by it. Then you understand why policemen laugh about the predicaments that people get themselves in and the pain and violence they bring on themselves. If you can't laugh about it, you will cry about it and be unable to do the job that has to be done."

Bill has heard most of this before as Pete's long-time friend.

"What a pain in the ass. I couldn't do it. I don't have the patience," he commented.

The neighbor chipped in. "Why do cops do what they do? Is it just a desire for power over people?"

"That's what a lot of people think about cops. A policeman understands the importance of his job too well. That's what makes it so hard on him. He sees the rotten part of our society and hopes and prays it will not affect his family or loved ones."

"We do have laws to take care of the bad guys, right?"

"Yeah, and when a good cop tries his best to do the job and gets his ass in a sling for doing it, it hurts." Pete was thinking of his current encounters with his job efforts.

"Why do you guys do it?"

"Sometimes I wonder, pal. But somebody's gotta do it, right?" The cigar and the beer tasted good to Pete.

Chapter Twenty-one

Ultimately, the Internal Affairs Division had to conclude that the allegations against Pete and Mel were "not sustained." IAD then sent the case back to the R&I Division for disposition. Pete was summoned into Captain Coy's office to hear his decision on the case that IAD had not been able to prove one way or the other. Pete's lieutenant was also present.

"Felix, IAD has sent this case back to me as 'not sustained.' What do you think is a fair adjudication for the complaint against you?" Pete couldn't resist this one.

"Well, Captain. I think a class A commendation would be appropriate."

"What! You're a real smart-ass, aren't you?"

"No, sir! I just think of what would have happened if Tennesen and I hadn't been there to help save this woman and get this bad guy off the street. Rampart fucked it up. Central Patrol fucked it up. IAD dove in and came up with a wet ass and no fish. I think the department should thank God for cops like Mel and me, who are still willing to do the job the way it's supposed to be done."

By now the captain was fuming and a little white residue of unknown substance had collected at the corner of his mouth.

"Well, you are gonna take a two-day suspension for neglect of duty and that's my decision," he blurted.

"Neglect of duty?" Pete reiterated. "Neglect of duty?" he now yelled. "How on earth were we neglecting our duty by responding to a call for help?"

"You are working warrant service, not on patrol. You shouldn't have gotten involved with a patrol function."

"What does this badge say, Captain?" Pete pulled his badge out and waved it in the air.

"Does it say Warrant Officer? No! It says Police Officer! Does the decal on the side of our car say Warrant Service Only? No! It says Los Angeles Police Department and To Protect and Serve!" Pete was on his feet now.

"I'm not takin' two days off or even one day off for doin' what I did. Neglect of duty my ass! If you ask me, I'll tell you who's neglecting their duty." The captain stood up.

"Get out of here, Felix! You're headed for a Trial Board!"

"Thank you, sir! I guess you're right." And he walked out of the captain's office.

Later that day, Pete had a chance to discuss the situation with his partner.

"You can do what you want, Mel, and I'll understand. Two days ain't nothin' but I'm not going for it! You and I are the good guys in this whole thing. IAD screwed with the damned case for months and then had to throw it out because they couldn't make a case out of it and now this dipshit captain wants to give us two days suspension for neglect of duty?"

"Yeah, but do you really want to take a Trial Board over two days?" asked Mel.

"You know, Mel, so many things have happened in the last few months. And the bad thing about it is they are things that make the LAPD look bad. There seems to be a lack of concern for what's right. The department seems to have the attitude that it is more important to be politically correct than to protect law-abiding citizens. And I'm catching hell for *my* so-called attitude! It's really depressing." Pete hung his head down and shook it.

"Maybe we can talk to someone upstairs and get it squelched," suggested Mel. "You know several people in high places, don't you?"

"Yeah, I've worked with a couple of guys in the old days that are 'up there.'"

It didn't seem like a bad idea at that, he thought. Most commanding officers wouldn't stick their own necks out over a two-day suspension but anything was worth trying at this point.

After unsuccessfully trying to get an audience with the chief, Pete finally got an appointment to see Commander Roger White. White had been Pete's partner for several months at Central Patrol back in the late 1950s.

"Hey, Pete. How's it going?" said the commander as Pete came into his office.

"Obviously, not too well, or I wouldn't be here bugging you about this." Pete then related his story and the actions of his captain.

"Do you really intend to go for a Trial Board over two days off?"

"If I have to, I will. Damn it, Roger! Can't you see how unfair this is?"

"Sure, but you know as well as I that the captains that sit on those boards are not going to rule in your favor over two days. They will back your captain's decision."

"Look, Roger, all through my career, I have fought the good fight. I've done a good job for the City of Angels. Hell, I've got the scars to prove it too! What's happening to the job nowadays is scary. The department doesn't back up its men anymore. Even when the men are right! Most cops I know can't wait to make rank and get off the street or retire when they get twenty years and twenty minutes on the job. That's where we're really needed! Most of the old-timers like us don't want to do police work either. When guys like Mel and me are willing to take action that's needed, we get rewarded with complaints from illegal aliens and stupid watch commanders who won't make their officers do the right thing."

"What do you want me to do, Pete?"

"Talk to the chief. Tell him our story and ask him to call off the wolves."

"Can't do it, Pete. Not for a two-day suspension anyway."

"Don't you understand, Roger? It's not the time off! It's the principles involved here. Why should Mel and I suffer while the Rampart dipshits skate?"

"I'm sorry, Pete. No deal. I guess I'm covering my own ass as well, but that's the way it is."

Pete left the office more determined than ever not to give in. Mel decided to stick it out as well, which made Pete feel a little better. The next step was to find someone to defend them at their Trial Board.

Chapter Twenty-two

A Trial Board was now inevitable. Pete and Mel were convinced their actions had been justified in light of the circumstances surrounding the plight of Mrs. Bordeaux and the failure of the Rampart officers to take appropriate action to protect her. They had taken a stand and refused to back down; now all they could do was wait and do their best to prepare their defense.

They went to Sergeant Tom Wade and asked him to represent them at their upcoming Trial Board. Wade was one of several officers on the department called Defense Reps, who defended officers who were facing internal trials. Officers were allowed to hire attorneys if they so chose, but most didn't.

Pete and Mel met with Wade on several occasions to develop their defense.

"Well, boys, what are you going to tell the board? I've read the reports and your accounts, and I agree that you are both getting the shaft. But you know as well as I that convincing three captains to take sides against another captain for a two-day suspension is a tough cookie to overcome." Wade waited for an answer.

"I've been trying to get all this straight in my mind and how to tell our story to the board. We need to convince them that what we did was a part of our job and not just something we did that was off the wall," said Pete.

"Yeah, but getting these captains to accept that is possible, but it would be a miracle if they would apply it in conflict with other commanders' orders for only a two-day suspension," Wade contended. "Two days is not worth the time for these guys to spend on it—will be their attitude, I think."

"So we gotta use a big stick to do it" was Pete's answer. "How do we do that?" asked Mel. Pete was feeling sorry that he ever got his partner into this mess, but then Pete remembered something he had read in the newspaper sometime ago.

"Do you remember a few months ago when the news media gave the chief hell for having too many officers inside and not enough out in the streets?" asked Pete.

"Yes, I remember. The chief responded by putting police and city decals on all plain cars that were not undercover. Then he put out a press release saying that now every police officer in the field could be identified, even in a plain vehicle. Then citizens could see them and call upon them if needed."

"Exactly," said Pete. "I wonder what a Trial Board would say about a captain who tries to penalize officers for neglect of duty while they were responding to the call of a citizen and the officers are in plain clothes and in a plain car with the decals on it the chief had ordered place there?"

"I think you may have something, Pete," smiled Wade.

"Sounds like you need to visit the library and find a copy of that article, huh?"

Pete went to the LA Public Library the next day. He asked a clerk for help in this "police matter." The clerk wasted no time in coming up with the article in the *LA Times* from a few months prior to Pete and Mel's incident. Pete photocopied the article. Now he had something to smile about.

"How are you taking all this, honey?" asked Noel as they ate dinner that night.

"Oh, I'm still trying to get a grip on reality, I guess. I think it's time for me to hang it up, baby."

Pete's wife knew how much her husband loved his job.

"Don't you think this will all pass?"

"I can't see much future in it. If I win, I'll lose. My captain will probably transfer me back to patrol out in the Valley somewhere. If I lose, he will be just as pissed off just because I went all the way with this." Pete paused in thought.

"Maybe I'm a dinosaur on the job. I hear that term a lot lately. Sometimes I think it's me that's changed, and other times I think the job has changed. Maybe it's both. Anyway, I'm looking around for a new career."

Now forty-three years old, Pete had been a cop since he was twenty-one. He didn't know much about any other job, but he remembered the words of an old veteran who was retiring and going to work in a new career field. He said that a cop that spends twenty years or more on the job should be able to do anything.

"Well, you know I'll support whatever you decide to do. And you must know how I've worried that you'd end up in the hospital or worse," she said. She reached across the table and held his hand. She knew it would be tough for him to quit, but she had hoped it would end soon anyway.

"I know a couple of retired cops who work security for movie jobs. They make good money. Maybe I'll see what's up with them. Or I have sixteen years of experience riding motorcycles. Maybe I could teach motorcycle riding. And I have that teaching credential I got from that UCLA class at the academy a few years ago. I could teach traffic violator schools like one of the guys I know."

"Whatever you decide to do is fine with me," said his wife. Pete bent over the table and kissed her softly.

"Thanks," he said.

The trial date came, and the two partners found themselves sitting behind a table with their defense rep. The board was presided over by three captains of police. Pete only knew one slightly. The other two were strangers to him. The prosecutor, a Lieutenant Wilder, introduced them.

Wilder was a jerk-off Pete had known from when he worked motors in Watts. During the Watts Riot of 1965, this lieutenant had proven to be arrogant and unable to use common sense. Even though he had no motor officer training, Wilder had "borrowed" one of the motor officer's motorcycles and helmet to ride around and "check out the area" around the Watts Station House, where the men had been kept in reserve. This was totally in violation of department policy that should have resulted in his own Trial Board. But he got away with it. Now he was the one at Internal Affairs who would do his best to get Pete and Mel punished for "Department Policy Violation!"

To Pete's surprise, one of the three captains was the commander over the Rampart Division's investigators. *That could be good or bad*, thought Pete.

The trial began by the reading of the charges against the two officers. They were that "while assigned to working the Warrant Detail, the officers left and neglected their primary duty and became involved unnecessarily in a patrol activity, resulting in a formal complaint."

"They make it sound like we really did something bad," Pete whispered to Wade.

Wade shook his head for Pete to shut up.

"How do the officers plead?" asked the prosecutor.

"Not guilty," advised Wade.

"Proceed," said the captain in charge of the hearing. Lieutenant Wilder then presented the case and called the supervisor of the Warrant Detail, Sergeant Wilson. This appeared to be his big chance to get even with Pete once and for all. Wilson proceeded to tell the board what a surly officer Pete was and about several incidents Pete had been involved in since he came to the detail. He went on to talk about the off-duty shooting involving Pete and the complaint from the West LA Station. He then made statements regarding Pete's general "bad attitude."

Wade asked the sergeant, "What does any of that have to do with these charges?"

"Well, it shows a pattern of lack of discipline," he answered.

"Has Officer Felix ever disobeyed an order, to your knowledge, Sergeant?"

"Well . . . no, but . . ." Wade cut him off.

"As Officer Felix's supervisor, are you responsible for his work reviews every six months?"

"That is correct," answered the sergeant.

"I show you this review dated approximately six months ago. Is this your report?" Wade handed the paper to the witness.

"Um. Well, yes it is."

"On this report, or any other report concerning Officer Felix, have you stated that he was anything other than a satisfactory worker or have you commented on what you just described as a lack of discipline?" Sergeant Wilson started to perspire.

"I don't recall writing it down, but I mentioned it to him on several occasions."

"So you have no written documentation that says Officer Felix was a 'bad officer,' isn't that true?"

"Yes, but he was . . ."

"That will be all, Sergeant," came a stern word from the lead captain of the board.

The next thing the prosecution brought up was really ridiculous. Pete had accepted the small old desk he had seen in the basement at Mrs. Bordeaux's apartment house one time when he and Mel were there. It was one she was going to throw out because it had a large burn spot on it. Pete asked if he could have it, thinking his wife could refinish it, so Mrs. Bordeaux gave the old desk to him. Noel had been able to sand most of the burn spot off and had completely refinished it and the desk now stood in their bedroom. How Pete's supervisor had heard about it; he didn't have a clue. He did know that what he had done was in no way illegal or unethical but was being presented as though it were.

Wade brought out that this was really stretching to find something that they could hang their hats on. Then he emphasized that this petty matter like the Wilson testimony had nothing to do with the charges being brought against the two officers.

Lieutenant Wilder then called the detective sergeant from Rampart who had approved the report taken by Rampart patrol officers regarding the assault on Mrs. Bordeaux and her tenant. He was the detective with whom Pete had argued about the decision to construe the assault as a misdemeanor rather than a felony. This had really been the thing that set off the chain of events leading to the complaint.

The detective sergeant testified that patrol officers had taken the crime report and had brought in a suspect whom he had interviewed. He felt the report warranted the decision of the city attorney to authorize prosecution and released the suspect. He said he had advised the officers to tell Mrs. Bordeaux to seek a complaint through the city attorney. Of course, by that time, the suspect, Rivera, had disappeared.

On cross-examination, Wade bored in. "Isn't it true that Officer Felix and you listened to the story of the victim as she related it on the phone?"

"Yes."

"And didn't you tell Officer Felix that you would have the report changed to reflect a felony crime report instead of a misdemeanor?"

"Well I, uh, I didn't say I would change it. I said I'd review it, and if it needed to be modified, I would do it."

"And did you modify it?"

"No. I didn't see the need to."

"May I see the report, please?" asked the captain from the Rampart detectives. He read quietly for a few minutes then said,

"Sergeant, would you please look at this report again."

The report was handed back to the detective. He read. "Yes, sir?"

"Sergeant, do you see the elements of a felony in that report?"

"Well, uh, I . . . uh . . . I guess so, sir."

"Well, do you or don't you?" he pushed.

"Yes, sir, I do."

"Thank you. You are dismissed."

"Gentlemen," began Wade, "it is pretty obvious that these officers were responding to a felony call from a person they knew from prior police contact. She trusted them and knew that they would not let her down, as did others on this department. I would now like to call a couple of defense witnesses.

"Proceed."

"I call Mrs. Cecil Bordeaux."

Mrs. Bordeaux had nothing but good things to say about Mel and Pete. She spoke of how her tenant had assaulted her and others in her apartment and how she was held against her will at knifepoint in the room she and another tenant were painting. She told how Joe Palmer, the tattoo man, had tried to come to her rescue, was driven off by the knife-wielding Rivera, was later arrested for a marijuana charge, and had left town, fearing the police could not protect him or her.

The next witness for the defense was the owner of the car agency across the street from the apartment buildings managed by Mrs. Bordeaux. He owned all three of those buildings and was a well-respected Los Angeles businessman. He was also a reserve deputy sheriff. He related how Mrs. Bordeaux had told him about how Mel and Pete had saved her life from Rivera. Then he said, "May I ask a question of the board?"

"Certainly, sir," said the presiding captain. "Go ahead."

"These officers saved this woman's life. So why are you trying to fuck over them?" The three captains all squirmed in their seats.

"Ah, hmm." The presiding captain cleared his throat. "I assure you we are just trying to find out the truth about this case, sir. Thank you for your testimony here, sir."

The captain then turned to Wade. "Is there is anything further, Sergeant?"

"Just one more thing, sir," said Wade. "We'd like to introduce this recent newspaper article by our chief of police regarding officers in unmarked police vehicles being available to answer citizen's calls for police service. He ordered that all plain police vehicles, not being used undercover, to have LAPD 'Protect and Serve' decals placed on the doors on both sides of the vehicles. You may remember it."

"We'll take it under advisement. Now, if there is no more testimony or questions, the board will be in recess until three o'clock this afternoon. At that time, we will render a decision in this case."

Pete, Mel and Wade headed up to the seventh floor to the police cafeteria. As they entered the cafeteria, Pete felt sick.

"If you guys don't mind, I'm going up to the academy. If you want to come along, Mel, that's okay." Mel declined, so Pete headed up to the academy to kill the two hours until the board reconvened at three.

After venting his feelings to his old partner, Ron Byron, from motors, Pete headed back to the PAB for the decision on their case. As he rode the elevator up to the fifth floor, he dreaded what might come next. *But like having to face criminals in the street, you gotta do it*, he thought.

Mel and Wade were standing outside the hearing room when he arrived.

"Glad you could make it," carped Wade.

"Wouldn't miss it for the world," lied Pete. Mel was his usual quiet self.

They entered the hearing room and sat down. The prosecutor was sitting there already. Pete really hated that asshole. Not just because he was doing what he was doing, but also because he had such an arrogant air about it.

The three captains entered the room and took their seats. The presiding captain spoke.

"After hearing all the testimony and reviewing all the evidence presented here, we find the officers not guilty of the offense charged. You officers are dismissed."

Breathing a sigh of relief, Pete and Mel stood up and shook hands then thanked and congratulated Sergeant Wade. Pete walked up to the presiding captain and offered his hand. The captain took it.

"Congratulations on your victory. We are sorry to have to put officers though these kinds of proceedings, but it is sometimes unavoidable."

"I appreciate the guts it took for you three to decide in our favor,' said Pete.

"Most captains would have given us the time off just to support another captain's orders. Thanks."

"I hope you won't come away from this discouraged about the job," said the captain.

"Sir, this is my last day on this job," Pete heard himself say.

"I hope it isn't because of this."

"How could you think that, sir?" said Pete, smiling.

Pete walked out into the hall to meet Mel. Standing with Mel was Lieutenant Wilder. As Pete walked up, Wilder put out his hand.

"Congratulations on winning your case, Felix." Pete ignored the hand.

"No thanks to you! You guys put on a bogus case and tried every dirty trick in the book to convict us! Well, you didn't. Wanna know why? Because you had no case in the first place! As far as I'm concerned, you can go fuck yourself, Lieutenant, sir! Let's go where there's better-smelling air, Melvin."

Epilogue

The next day found Pete in the Personnel Division, talking to the retirement advisor. It took two days to review and sign all the papers for retirement. A sad business. But on the good side, Pete had received an offer of employment from a large motorcycle manufacturing company where several of his retired buddies were now employed. The job involved motorcycle safety instruction and it sounded challenging and exciting. He knew he would suffer withdrawals from the police department, but it had to be. His wife was happy about his decision.

On his last day in the Warrant Detail Office, he said good-bye to the troops. He wondered if any of his supervisors would come down to send him off. None did.

As he walked out of the PAB for the last time as a cop, he thought about Mel. He would have to get himself a new partner. He hoped he'd find one that didn't like to drive. He thought about Sherry Barone and her mother and wondered if Sherry would end up the same. He thought about assholes like Julio Rivera and Ronald the Woman Beater and all the others he had tried to help, or put in jail, over the years. The adjustment to civilian status was going to be hard. Once a cop, always a cop, they say.

The men with whom Pete had worked in the Warrant Detail gave him an off-duty retirement party, which his supervisors had refused to give him, at a local Mexican restaurant. That was enough for Pete.

And, he wondered, *what about the hide-and-seek game?* It will go on and probably get worse. In a county with about nine million people and millions of warrants for arrests issued, only twelve men of the LAPD were trying to serve them; it could only get worse. Officers in the field were being deterred from running people through the computer system to find wanted suspects. Management seemed to think that keeping them on the streets was more important than making the criminals pay for their actions.

No one in governmental authority seemed to take notice of the millions of dollars in fines that were being ignored. The criminals learn soon that the chances of getting caught after jumping bail or failing to show up for trial are slim. Pete took comfort in the fact that when he and Melvin were on the street, the odds for the criminal were not as good.

So he reconciled himself to a couple of facts that he already knew from past experience but didn't like to admit. One; there is life after the police department, and two; things are the way they are and a cop can do little about it because . . . that's the way it is!

The End